JESSICA WATKINS PRESENTS

LONG AS
YOU
KNOW WHO YOU
Belong To III

BRI NOREEN

Acknowledgements

I'm going to keep this short and sweet. A special thanks to God because Lord knows I needed all the strength to get through this third book. I'm in awe that I have a full finished series! This is the first story that I have EVER finished so I'm super proud of myself.

Thanks to all my sisters in pen, you know who you are. A special thank you to Jasmine and Perri. Your encouragement and help with this book was greatly appreciated. Thank you to my reader's group on FB and the others that I pop in occasionally. Also a special, special thanks to Tee Sherrod. You'll see why.☺ Thank you to the readers who have hung with me while I got my life together and took FOREVA (Cardi B voice) to get book three out. Ya'll are amazing!

With no further ado....

LONG AS
YOU
KNOW WHO YOU
Belong To **III**

Previously in Long As You Know Who You Belong To 2....

Kimani
August 2015

"Fuck, fuck, fuck, fuck, FUCK!" I groaned to myself.

Today should have been the happiest day of my life. Instead, it was clouded with more bullshit than I could handle. Blu was back. The moment she came strutting into the club, the heaviness in my heart released. I felt like a weight had been lifted from my shoulders. I could finally breathe. That feeling was short-lived once Blu told me what she had been up to the past few months. After she had given me all the details behind her fake death, I knew that Grey and I were screwed. It was like the shit was never ending!

I had to get to my brother before shit began to really get fucked up. As I made my way to him, my eyes darted back and forth to the clock. I had been holding onto something that would probably fuck his and my relationship up completely; but more importantly, it could possibly be the very thing that ended his life. After I got a hotel room for Blu an hour away from the city, I hopped in my whip and gunned it to Grey's crib.

Karma
August 2015

Tonight was the night that I would make my move. I was finally going to get my revenge. Nine had come through with her people just like she said she would. We were going to get that muthafucka so that I could fuck up his world. Oh, how fucking sweet it would be to see the look on his face when he realized that a bitch wasn't really dead. Just the thought was better than any orgasm, present, or shopping spree a simple bitch could dream of.

I felt bad for leaving Roman behind after all that he had done for me, but fuck him right now. He was doing too much anyway. All that planning and exacting revenge he'd done, and nothing had gone right. He was back at square one. I didn't have another two years to sit around twiddling my thumbs to come up with another half-baked plan that was bound to fail. I finally had to admit to myself, that the 'team' thing was never really my forte. I was an independent bitch who worked better alone, and my current situation proved it. I was going to get this muthafucka while Roman's ass was somewhere twisting in the wind. I was sad that I would have to let the dick go, but good dick wasn't hard to find; and once I tortured and killed Grey, I would start my manhunt.

I sat in the car waiting for Nine to hop back in. She had run in the gas station over five minutes ago. Just when I was about to get out and go looking for the bitch, she eased back in the whip.

"Alright, let's go," she said. I put the key in the ignition and pulled off in the direction of Grey's home. "Remember, move on my command. Don't do nothing crazy."

I didn't even respond. I just drove without saying anything. Somebody should've told that bitch. My middle name *was* crazy.

Roman
August 2015

"You got everything?" I asked Israel.

"Stop checking my every move, nigga. We're good."

We were done wasting time. This fuck nigga was getting bodied tonight. We had done enough stalling and planning. I had been investing time and money into taking everything from that nigga and making him suffer. I wanted to strip him of everything and everyone that made him who he was. That's the revenge I really wanted—for him to know how it felt to fucking lose. My family meant everything to me, and I had lost everything in one swoop because a snitch nigga couldn't do his fucking time. I strongly believed that the punishment should fit the crime, but at this point, I didn't have the fucking energy to start all over. Taking his life was going to have to be enough.

The plan was to run up on this nigga at his crib and body him. It was the place where he was most vulnerable and had the least amount of security. Because of his recent trip to Atlanta to check on that old bitch, we were able to infiltrate his security system. We placed coded viruses in his electronic system that we could activate remotely, and at any moment. Those viruses would allow us access to his crib without him even knowing that his security had been breached. It was a backup plan that we had initiated, but at least that part of the plan still was going to come in handy.

We had also been tracking his movements via the GPS on his car, and according to what I was looking at, he was headed home now. If we left immediately, we would catch him before he stepped foot in his crib. Pussy nigga just ain't know it was his last day breathing. Hope the nigga had enjoyed a good-ass day.

Blaze
August 2015

I couldn't believe what I had found out. Initially, I thought I was crazy for trying to piece together the motive behind Roman's obsession with taking Grey down because I had no clue where to start. But when you're backed up against the wall, your brain works in overdrive to get out of the tough spot. I had reached out and asked for favors from people I barely knew and spent my day running around town like a madwoman, but it was worth it because I'd found answers. I knew that there was still a good chance that I was going to have to tell Grey about my past, but I was more willing to lay my past at his feet if I could offer him something that could possibly save his life. I just hoped that he loved me enough to look past my faults.

As I turned down Grey's street, I got a funny feeling in the pit of my stomach. I couldn't tell if I really sensed that something wasn't right or if I was nervous about what I had to tell him, but I shook it off and pulled into the driveway. Throwing my hoodie over my head to shield myself from the light drizzle that had started to pour, I hopped out of the car and made my way toward the house.

Grey
August 2015

My eyes shot open as my body tensed and my hands gripped the couch cushions beside me. I was dripping in sweat, but a cold chill still managed to slither up my spine as I reflected on the nightmare that I had just awakened from. Secure with the fact that I was in my home and not in front of my restaurant like my dream led me to believe, I buried my head in my hands and breathed a sigh of relief. That shit had me fucked up real quick. It had felt so real that I damn near felt the bullet pierce my side as I stood on the red carpet holding Blaze's hand. The craziest shit was seeing Nakami so vividly. She looked different but phenomenal for a bitch that was supposed to have died in a fucking house fire.

"The fuck?" I mumbled aloud.

I couldn't believe I was seriously getting myself worked up over a dream about a chick I knew for a fact was nothing but bones and ashes. The dream was too real for me not to trip. With the grand opening being less than ten days away, my dumb ass actually believed that that night had already come, and it had me hyperventilating and shit. Shaking the dream off, I stood from the couch and wiped my face with my hand. A nigga really needed to get it together. But the dream was nagging me. Ma Dukes had always told me that dreams that you remember are always remembered because your subconscious is trying to tell you something. So what was it that my subconscious was trying to tell me?

While I traveled from the living to the kitchen, the sound of the door opening, caused me to negate the thoughts running through my head and look in that direction with anticipation. I knew that it could only be my baby, so I continued walking toward the front door to greet my boo. She was just coming into the house, front door ajar, dressed casually in a baggy sweat suit with the hood up. She smiled when she saw me.

"Hey, fiancé," she grinned.

She slipped off her shoes as we walked towards one another, but our greeting was interrupted as the ear popping sounds of gunshots rang out. Bullets flew through the windows and doors, breaking every barrier they traveled through and sending remnants of glass, wood and debris flying everywhere. I hit the floor, and I told Blaze to do the same. The shots rang out for what felt like forever. I scrambled to get to my strap, and when I got it, I started busting back at them niggas. The only problem was, it felt like the shots were surrounding us. It was like they weren't just coming from one direction. I ducked back down when I realized I was out of rounds and tried to make my way back to Blaze. By the time I got back to the hallway, the gunshots had stopped, and I could hear a car skid off in the distance. Panic struck me instantly, and I ran to Blaze to help her as I saw her face down on the floor.

"B! You good?! B?!" I yelled out to her as I tried to turn her over. "Aww man! No, man! B! Blaze, baby. Hold on, B!" I cradled her head in my lap and stared at the bullet hole in her chest. She looked at me with wide eyes as she tried to breathe. "Baby, please!"

I didn't know what the emotion was that was brewing inside of me as I looked at her, but that shit was lethal. I couldn't think straight. My mind was all fucked up. If Blaze didn't fucking make it, I was liable to kill everything moving until the pain went away! "Fuck!" I yelled, as I frantically applied pressure to the wound and looked her in her eyes as I used my free hand to dial 911.

"B, stay with me, baby. You've gotta make it. Cuz if you don't..." I bit down on my lip as I struggled to continue. "...Cuz If you don't, I'm snatching the soul of everyone they have ever loved, cared for or even came in fucking contact with. I promise that."

LONG AS YOU KNOW WHO YOU BELONG TO III

Grey
August 2015

I walked into the dimly lit restaurant with fury rushing through my body. The thesaurus didn't hold a word deadly enough to describe the emotion that I was feeling, but the fuck niggas that put me in this situation were going to be immersed in the consequences of their actions sooner rather than later. I walked into the main area of After Midnight where in less than a week, a celebration was supposed to take place. Now that shit would be put on hold. Looking around at the team assembled in front of me, I felt a brief sense of relief. My best move yet had been to bring my niggas from the D out west, because if I hadn't needed them before, I definitely needed them now and I knew my crew was thorough enough to get shit done.

Dressed in all black and ready to wage war, my family sat around waiting for me to give the word. Kimani, Brandin, Cope, Treach, Keem, Onyx, Martine, Dustin, Mhizani, Simba, Ryan, Bailey, Erika, Seven and Jah all looked at me; their expressions mirroring the rage that was emanating from my body. I opened my mouth to speak but quickly closed it. I had never felt emotion this vividly before to the point where I couldn't control myself or my body. But seeing Blaze laid out like that, gushing blood, had me in a murderous rage. Taking a deep breath, I made another attempt to speak.

"We were violated today," I said, struggling to stay strong. "Some fuck ass niggas decided to try me, and now my fiancé is in the hospital fighting for her life. I know that those muthafuckas, Israel, and Roman Nueva are the ones responsible. My guess is that they think that I'm in some way responsible for how shit went down with the FEDS and the death of their father."

I scanned the room and watched as my soldier's faces contorted with wrath. I could damn near see their hearts turn black with vengeance. They felt my pain, and I had complete confidence that they would come through for a nigga. It wasn't just a statement when I said that we were family. As far as I was concerned, every person in this room was blood relatives, and no DNA test could tell me any different.

"Now I don't give a fuck how we get to these muthafuckas or who gets to them first, but I want them brought to me alive. You have my permission to kill any and everyone that stands in your way or has ties to these niggas. And if Blaze don't make it..." I got choked up just thinking that there was a possibility that Blaze wouldn't be okay.

Sensing that I was struggling with the words, Brandin spoke up. "We got you, nigga. Say no more," he said.

Collective head nods were seen around the room, and I returned the sentiment. I couldn't say more, or I would break down, so I opted to just walk away. Before I got to the back door, I felt a hand on my shoulder. I turned around and saw that it was Kimani.

"What's up, bruh?" I said, exasperated. I was ready to get back to the hospital and was hoping that whatever he had to tell me could wait.

"I gotta holla at you. Some shit I gotta say that…"

I cut him off. "Can it wait? B is probably in surgery and…"

"It can't wait."

I looked at him, and I was sure that he could see the weariness in my eyes. I couldn't handle no more bullshit tonight. I had been ambushed in my own home, my fiancé had been shot, and I had found out that I had two enemies on my head. But as I stared at Kimani, I could tell that whatever he had to say to me was important, so I released a sigh and nodded. Fuck else could go wrong?

Kimani
August 2015

I was nervous as fuck about what I needed to get off my chest. I had done some stupid shit in my life, but this by far had to have been the most reckless shit I had ever involved myself in. I had let emotions cloud my judgment and what I had done was finally coming back to haunt me. *Fuck.* I watched as the last of Grey's crew exited the restaurant, in no way anxious to have this conversation with my brother. The door at the front of the restaurant slammed signaling that we were now alone. Grey shoved his hands down in his pockets and took the deepest sigh known to man. With heavy-lidded eyes, he looked up at me.

"What's up, Mani?" he queried.

I knew the answer to the question, but I asked anyway. "So these niggas that's after you are Jorge's sons?"

"Apparently," he responded, simply.

"And they after you because they think that you had something to do with the FEDS coming after they pops?"

"Bro, what do you got to say? I ain't got time for you to be fucking beating around the bush." Irritation laced his voice. "Spit that shit out."

"Aight man. Look, so remember when Ginae was killed?"

He squinted in confusion. He was probably wondering what Ginae had to do with what was happening now. I wasn't looking forward to telling him, but I had to. I closed my eyes, willing the night that Ginae was shot to replay in my mind.

June 2012

"Urgghhhhh!" I screamed before my fist connected with the dingy white wall inside the hospital emergency room. Physical and emotional pain engulfed me as the doctor's words continued to swirl around in my mind.

"We did everything we could...she lost too much blood....if it had entered a little to the left..."

I had picked up little pieces of what the doc had said, but it all amounted to the same thing. Because of the shit that I was involved in, my girl had lost her life. She was bright and funny and had a fucking future outside of the hood, but I had put her in harm's way. I was going to be the reason that her momma had to make funeral arrangements. Tears sprang from my eyes as I thought about how her death would affect her family and friends. The shit was my fault, man. No, I hadn't pulled the trigger, but I had put her in the midst of my bullshit, and she had paid the ultimate price.

"Kimani Summers?" a voice behind me spoke.

Thinking that it was the doctor again, I pulled myself up off the floor and turned around. I was greeted by a tall, lanky white man dressed in a suit and a decent looking black chick wearing the same getup. Immediately my face scrunched because I just knew these pigs weren't expecting me to talk to *them about shit after my girl had just died. These niggas had no fucking respect.*

"I ain't talking to no police." I brushed them off and began to walk away.

The white nigga spoke. "We aren't the police, and we aren't asking."

Out of curiosity, I turned around. "'Scuse you?"

The black lady stepped up and held out her identification. "My name is Agent Falise Wyatt and this is Agent Brody Dunn. We're from the DEA's office, and we need to have a word with you about Kendrick Summers."

"The DEA, nigga? What the fuck?" Grey interrupted my story with his outburst. "You never told me shit about you being approached by the fucking boys!"

"Are you going to let me finish the story, nigga? This is hard enough as it is."

Grey didn't say anything, but the look he shot me let me know that it was okay to continue.

I wasn't sure what the DEA knew about my brother and our illegal activity but the fact that they had come to me first, lead me to believe that they didn't know much. Figuring that I could give Grey a heads up based on the shit they wanted to talk to me about, I agreed to sit down with them. We walked out of the emergency room and to a secured part of the hospital. They ushered me into a small office and motioned for me to have a seat. The female agent clicked on a recorder and set it on the desk before she turned to me.

"Yo, I need a lawyer or something? What the fuck you recording me for?"

"It's up to you if you want to get a lawyer. But once you do that, we can't help you," Agent Wyatt stated.

"Help me with what, man? I ain't done shit."

"Son, it's in your best interest to be cooperative here."

I hopped up from my seat and headed towards the door. "I ain't your GODDAMN SON! Yo, I'm out."

"We've been looking at your brother and his organization for the last couple months, Kimani."

A cold chill slithered down my spine at Agent Dunn's words. I stopped in my tracks trying to calm my breathing. I couldn't let this nigga see me sweat. I turned back around.

My best bet was to play dumb. "What organization, sir?" I asked, with a smirk.

"Kimani, you can act like you don't know anything about the drugs that your brother sells, the bodies that his band of thugs have collected, or even that you haven't been his right-hand man...but we know about it. We are this close to moving in on him and figured that you would want to help yourself."

The thought of betraying my brother to save my own ass made my skin crawl. I wasn't no fucking snitch, and I definitely wasn't giving my blood fucking brother up to get away with some shit we had entered together. I wasn't built like that. Before I could respond, Agent Wyatt continued.

"You have a future ahead of you, Kimani. Not to say that Kendrick couldn't have had one as well, but he's too deep into this to have anything tangible. You—you've had minimal contact with moving weight and any of the murders that we can connect to your brother, so it's likely you could get out of this with minimal time to serve."

"Man, ya'll ain't got shit on me or my brother. I'm not stupid, so you're going to have to come harder than that if you're going to convince me that we're actually in some real trouble."

Agent Dunn went over to the table in the corner and pulled a folder out of a leather bag, and smirked as he handed it to me. I flipped it open, and once I saw what was inside, I swallowed all the arrogance that I had previously displayed. There were pictures of Grey at our shipment drops meeting with our team and one of him meeting with the niggas that were responsible for the shootout that had ended Ginae's life. These niggas were telling the truth. They had been on to us for months. To see that they really had a case against my brother knocked the wind out of me. I couldn't let him go to jail.

"Mannn..." I started, as I tossed the folder onto the desk. It missed by a few inches, and all of the pictures fell out and onto the floor. One picture in particular fell and caught my eye. Agent Wyatt kneeled down with an irritated sigh to pick them up, but I stopped her.

"Wait," I requested, grabbing up the picture that had landed by her feet.

I studied the photo as my mind raced. I had to do something, right? What kind of brother was I if I wasn't my brother's keeper? If I had the ability to save my brother's life, I would do it in a heartbeat. True, I was pissed that our bullshit had put Ginae in the line of fire and cost her her life, but that nigga was still my brother. Everything in my heart blamed him for the way that things had turned out. His hotheaded ass was the reason them niggas came at us and ultimately the reason why I was mourning the loss of my girlfriend, but I would die trying to protect him.

"Him...what if I gave you him for Gre—Kendrick's and my freedom?" I spoke as I pointed at the man in the photo.

Dunn and Wyatt balked. Dunn snatched the picture from my hand and looked at it closely before he responded.

"Jorge. Jorge Nueva? Son, you've gotta come with
something better than that. He's untouchable. We've been
trying to bring him down for years. And if a whole task force
failed to do it, I'm sure what little contact you've had with him
won't help us catch him."

"He's our connect. And we have unrequited access to him.
I can tell you where he rests his head, the names of that
nigga's dogs and outline the coca field where he grows his
product."

It was true. We had linked up with Jorge a few years ago,
and he had taken us in like sons. He invited us to parties,
showed us the process of breaking down the coca leaves, and
we'd toured his home on numerous occasions. It was a
betrayal, sure, knowing how close Jorge was with us, but Grey
was blood, and if I had to choose between Grey being locked
up or ratting out Jorge, the choice was easy. Damn, didn't I
just say I wasn't a snitch? Spoke too soon.

"If you can give us Jorge we will let you and your brother
be. I mean it's not like your brother will be able to continue his
business if we take Jorge down, so we could back off to catch
the big fish," Agent Wyatt mused.

I looked between Agent Wyatt and Agent Dunn as they
mulled the idea over, praying like hell they took my offer.
Putting Grey out of business for a while could be beneficial.

Maybe he would start taking care of his legit businesses and get out of the drug game for good. Me? I was on the first thing smoking after I laid Ginae to rest. I was done with the drug game regardless of how minimal my role was. This shit wasn't worth it to me. I looked up at Agent Wyatt as a grin eased across her face.

"You got yourself a deal."

As soon as the last word came out my mouth, I felt the force of Grey's fist collide with my jaw. I was surprised, but that didn't stop me from hemming that nigga up against the wall. I knew he was mad. And I knew he was *going* to be mad when I told him that I was the one that had sent the boys after Jorge, killed his illegal business in Detroit and ultimately played a hand in the reason why Jorge's sons were coming after him, but he wasn't about to beat my ass.

"You snitched?!" Grey yelled. The bass in his voice rattled the pictures that were hung on the walls around us. He pushed me off him angrily. "You gave up Jorge?!"

"I did it for you!" I yelled back. "They had enough shit on you to have your yellow ass doing twenty-five to life, nigga!"

Before I knew it, Grey was coming at me like a fucking linebacker. He rushed me and rammed my body into the nearest table. The chairs went flying every which way as we crashed onto the floor. I scrambled to get up as Grey untangled himself from the mess of broken furniture he had landed in.

"Blaze might die because of you!" He launched his fist near my face, but I was quick enough to avoid it.

Grey was fighting with bottled up emotions and wasn't nearly as dangerous with his hands at the moment as he was trained to be. Lunging for his torso, I tackled him back down to the floor. Out of breath and out of fight, I rolled over trying to control my breathing.

"And I lost Ginae because of you. Now we're almost even, nigga."

I was over his 'woe is me' bullshit. This nigga had done plenty of dirt and ultimately he knew that with the lifestyle that he lived, losing someone he loved was always a possibility. True, I had set the wheels in motion when I gave the DEA information on Jorge but knowing the shit that had gone down with Ginae, he should have had more presence of mind to keep Blaze safe and away from the bullshit. He wasn't going to place all the blame on me. Slowly, I stood up as Grey remained on the floor running his hands over his now loose dreads.

"Look, man, I couldn't have known that this was the way that things were going to turn out. We didn't even know that

Jorge had any sons!" I waited for Grey to speak, but he was silent. "Grey, I know you mad…"

He stood up from the floor causing me to grow quiet. I watched as he brushed the debris from his clothes and pulled his hair back into the ponytail. He walked off towards the door without looking at me.

"Grey! Grey, man you just not gon' say nothing?!"

Grey turned around slowly. The weariness that he felt was evident; in his eyes and in his posture. He looked as though he had been hit by the force of a Mack Truck, then ran over and dragged for a couple miles. I felt fucked up. I had never meant to hold on to this secret so long, or for it to cause so much damage. At the time, I honestly thought I was doing the best thing for the both of us.

"Fuck you what me to say? Huh?" His voice cracked. "This shit fucked up. If B dies, man…"

"She won't."

"I hope not. Because if she dies, you're dead to me too."

His words shocked the hell out of me. I opened my mouth to say something but thought better of it. I knew that shit was his anger talking and that he needed some time. I watched as he walked out of the restaurant and hopped in his car. Silently, I prayed to God that Grey would forgive me. My brother and I had gotten back to the relationship we'd once had, and I didn't want this shit to be the reason that we fell off again. Shaking myself off, I walked out of the restaurant and locked up. Sliding into my car, I made up my mind that I would do whatever I needed to do to find these fuck niggas for Grey. I was hopeful that Blaze would pull through, but if she didn't, I would kill Roman and Israel myself. I had to have my brother's back right now because I was all he had.

Karma
August 2015

"You want to tell me what the fuck that shit was about?" I poked my hip out and anchored my hand on it.

"Fuck are you talking about, Nakami?" Nine rolled her eyes in irritation.

"Don't call me that shit! My name is Karma!" I screamed.

"If you don't calm your retarded ass down." She waved me off as she sat down at the hotel desk that was situated near the floor to ceiling window. "I didn't like that old fortune cookie ass name anyway. That was all Hero's idea."

I groaned. This bitch was going to drive me crazy as If I wasn't already there. Flopping down on the bed, I eased out of my black Timbs. Our plan had not gone as expected. We had pulled up near Grey's house and had positioned our people around the perimeter, waiting for Nine to give us the go ahead. We were going to shoot through the windows, go in and snatch his ass. I had a nice little workspace all set up to torture his ass in after we grabbed him up. But shit went left before we even got a chance to get into the house. Out of nowhere, gunshots had gone off. We ducked for cover, hurried back into the car and got the fuck outta dodge. Unless there was someone else after that nigga, I knew that the shooters had to be Roman and his people. He was going to be an issue. His plan had gone to shit, and now he was grasping at straws, and it was fucking with my plans.

"So what's your next move, Karma?" Nine rolled her eyes when she said my name.

"First, I need to know if that nigga is still alive. The way those gunshots popped off, I'd be surprised if he wasn't at least injured. Guess I need to go by the hospital and see what's going on." I huffed.

"Well, you're on your own. You got the block hot with all that shoot 'em up cowboys shit you had me trying to pull so I need to lay low for a while. Tomorrow morning I'll be gone."

"Good," I mumbled.

As good of a front I was putting up, I was hurt at the fact that I had just gotten my mother back in my life and not only was the bitch leaving after a week, but she had no desire to try and build a relationship with me. I had once longed for a mother, and now that I had her she didn't want to be bothered. She had played the part of egg donor and wiped her hands of me. Shit hurt like a mug, but I refused to let on.

"I'm still keeping that money you gave me. My fee is non-refundable."

Nine stood and pulled her hair back into a ponytail. Like the gazelle that she was, she swiftly crossed the room and entered the bathroom, closing the door behind her. I let my body fall back onto the bed as my legs dangled from the edge. This was all a bunch of bullshit. I was holding on to so much hate that I couldn't even think straight at the moment. I hated everything and everybody. I hated Grey for turning my life upside down. I hated Blu for being a little dick-bouncing whore and fucking the only man that ever made me feel complete. I hated Nine for being a cold-hearted bitch who wanted to have nothing to do with the child that she birthed. I hated Roman for being a soft pansy, pussy ass nigga and letting his extravagant planning get in the way of the objective; killing Grey. I hated Blaze's 'two peppermints away from being obese' ass for stealing my got damn man! I hated all these muthafuckas!

I used to be happy, running my business, keeping myself fly, partying with my best friend and chilling with my father. Now, because of all the shit heads listed above, my life was ruined. My father was dead, everyone thought *I* was dead, My business was shut down. I was running out of money and options, and I had no idea what my next move was. As I felt sleep raining down on me like pixie dust, my mind carried thoughts of how to end all my problems once and for all. I was gunning for each and every single life that had a hand in ruining mine, and I wasn't going to stop until I tasted blood for every sin cast against me. Niggas owed me for what they took away, and they were going to pay with their lives.

Roman
August 2015

"FUCK!" I roared.

My normally light brown skin had turned a deep shade of crimson as I let the anger I was feeling bubble up to the surface. *How had the plan gone so fucking wrong?* This shit was supposed to be simple. I had everything planned down to the letter and nothing had gone right. Even our last ditch efforts had failed because we got to the party too late and weren't able to catch that nigga slipping like we had hoped. Turns out the person we had been following was his bitch, Blaze and she was the one that had taken the slugs meant for him. I was disgusted with myself. I was the fucking son of Jorge Nueva, goddamit! And I couldn't even get rid of one bum ass nigga. I had to get my shit together. Sitting down in the office chair behind my desk, I let my face sink into my hands.

"What do we do now?" Israel asked.

I had forgotten he was in the room until I heard his voice bounce off the walls. I groaned because I didn't have the patience to deal with my twin right now. I was the brains behind this shit, and he was the muscle. He was looking to me for instructions and at the moment, I didn't have any. I didn't even know where to fucking start.

"I don't know, bro."

"I honestly think we should let this shit go. It's causing more problems than we need and---"

I bolted out of my chair and into Israel's face. I was so pissed off at his suggestion that I was practically foaming at the mouth.

"Let it go? LET IT GO?!" I screamed. "Our father is fucking dead! And our sister is a fucking vegetable because of him! We lost everything! Every fucking thing because that bitch made nigga couldn't do his time! And you want me to let shit go?!"

With tremendous force, Israel pushed me out of his face. I stumbled back, hitting the edge of the desk but caught myself before I hit the ground. The anger in Israel's eyes stopped me from retaliating. He was really feeling some type of way right now.

"I'm just saying; we running out of money chasing behind this stupid nigga. And for what? If we get a hold of this nigga, then what? Is he going to magically make Pops reappear? Is his death going to make Italia wake the fuck up? No, nigga! So what are we doing this for?"

"Because he fucking violate—"

"Ain't that a risk of the game?" Israel asked, cutting me off. "I'm sure pops didn't think that he was invincible. That's apparent by the way he stashed money away for us. Killing muthafucka's and kidnapping people is some ol' Mob shit! We ain't the Mob! Before Pops died, I fought him tooth and nail to stay away from his empire and now I'm helping you avenge it?" He spoke with exasperation.

"That's all we got left of him, nigga! The fuck you mean?" I was back in my brother's face with spittle flying like snowflakes. "We them niggas, now! Because of that ingrate, we have to start from the fucking bottom to rebuild our father's legacy. And he's supposed to just go on his merry way? We supposed to just let that shit slide because that's a risk of the game? That was our fucking father!"

I lost my breath as my emotions got the best of me. Just thinking about the fact that the nigga that raised us to be the men we are was never going to see us live out his dream, made me physically sick to my stomach. The fact that there was nothing that I could do to aid in the bettering of my sister's health crushed me. I felt weak and incompetent even though in the back of my mind I knew that these were situations I had no control over. I was supposed to protect my family as a man, and I didn't have the power to do anything to make it right. I couldn't understand why Israel couldn't see this was the only way that I could make things better.

"But killing other niggas ain't gon' bring him back to life. Look, man; I get it. You hurt. You think I ain't hurt? I am. And this is crazy to me that I'm even saying this to you because I'm normally the wild boy, but nigga you're too far gone. You obsessed with this nigga and that shit is going to be your downfall."

"*Your*? Fuck you saying, yo? You out?"

Israel looked at me, his eyes full of regret and defeat. I knew what he was getting at but I refused to accept it.

"I'm done. I always got your back but this...this shit here is going to be the death of you. All that talk about legacy and you making moves that's going to put you in a position to not even be able to carry the name on. I'm sorry, bro. I can't do it."

With that, Israel opened the door and walked out without even glancing back. I stared at the door for a few moments as rage started to fill my body like a syringe and I erupted. All the shit that had previously been on my desk went flying through the air, landing in disarray across my office. I was fuming! If Israel had thought that him leaving me hanging was going to make me reconsider, he was sadly mistaken. His betrayal had only gotten me more amped.

None of this shit would have happened it if hadn't been for Grey. I was on a war path to destroy him no matter what the cost. Oh, and Karma? I was going to get that bitch too.

Israel
August 2015

I walked over to my silver 2016 Maserati Levante and sighed before reaching out to open the door. I was used to luxury like this, but the way that my brother was blowing money like it grew on trees had me worried about the future of my spending. Sliding into the butterscotch leather driver's seat, I cranked up the car and put it in drive, calculating my next move.

I needed to find some fucking independence. All my life I was bound to another muthafucka in one way or another. First had to walk around with the heaviness of my father's name weighing on my back and to top that off, I shared the same face as another nigga. Don't get me wrong; I loved my brother, but I was starting to feel like I was suffocating. Every time I turned around, I was being forced into something because of my family or my family's namesake. But what about what I wanted to do? I didn't want any parts of supplying drugs, and I definitely didn't want to spend the rest of my life looking for ways to get back at another nigga. I wanted peace. And right now, there was only one thing that gave me peace. Blu.

I knew that it was a bad idea to agree to all this bullshit my brother had cooked up, but I was indebted to him. I used to be a major fuck-up; always running off emotions and never off common sense. I had caught bodies for the simplest shit, feeling like the world owed me something, and my brother was always there to have my back and to cover up my messes. I was a young, wild nigga who'd known how to handle a gun since the age of 10 and goddamnit if the only thing that had ever calmed me down was a bitch.

My life hadn't been the same since Blu had entered it. Just her presence alone had slowed a niggas heart down from its irregular tempo, and she had calmed me in ways nothing and no one had ever been able to. Trust and believe I still had my moments, but she made me gentle and thoughtful. If we had met under different circumstances, it would have been nothing for me to cop a diamond and give her my last name. But being the nigga who had basically kidnapped her and trained her to kill, I held out little hope for a happy ending.

She'd disappeared before we went on our final mission to get at Grey and I knew by now that she had to know the truth about what had happened. And if that was the case, I had the slimmest chance known to man, to make things right and win her back. But I was determined to make whatever chance I had count. I wasn't sure what the fuck I was going to do or how I was going to find her, but I wasn't giving up until I had given it my best effort. So fuck Roman and his dumb ass plan right now. If I didn't find Blu and get her back, I didn't know what was liable to happen to my heart. She had managed to tame the beast but without her here to keep him locked down, I couldn't guarantee that he would stay away for long.

Blu
August 2015

Big, bold water droplets fell from the rainfall shower head in the massive glass-enclosed shower, but they did little soothe me. My mind was running a million miles a minute as I tried to piece together the puzzle that had become my life. The shit that Kimani had dropped on me floored me and pissed me off. I didn't know who to trust. I had been shacking up with a man that I thought I loved for almost a year, and it turned out he was out to cause me harm. Or was he? Kimani claimed to have my best interest at heart but honestly I didn't know him either. Who was telling the truth?

I sighed and placed my head in my hands. Feeling the prune-like texture of my fingernails reminded me that I had been standing under the water way longer that I had anticipated and needed to get my shit together. I reached out and turned the shower off by its digital remote and stepped out.

"Shit!" I screamed, nearly jumping out of my skin when I saw him.

I opened my mouth to curse him out for scaring me, but he covered my lips with his instead. *This.* Our connection was what made me want to believe every word he said wholeheartedly. I felt his soul when our lips touched, and my heart leapt so fast and so furious that it almost exited my chest. As soon as or bodies met, a transference of energy occurred. I could feel that something was wrong with him. He was in pain, and I could feel it. And instinctively, I wanted to be the one to take it away.

Stark naked and covered in water, I pressed my body against his fully clothed one and melted into him. His large hands squeezed my body with the force of a man molding clay and his tongue danced with angst inside my mouth. How could I feel so connected to him but not remember this? Remember him? Where my brain was struggling to put together images of us in my head, my body had no issues remembering what he was capable of. I was raining love juice in the same manner that the shower head had just rained over me, and all we were doing was kissing.

Pulling his snapback from his head and placing it on the sink behind him, Kimani hoisted me up by waist and wrapped my legs around him. He used his well-toned, tatted arms to pull my body even closer to him and deepen the kiss. Grabbing the sides of his head, I forced him to open his eyes and look at me. I wanted to get lost in the emerald city that was his eyes. The intensity, lust, and love that emanated from them almost caused my impending orgasm to burst from my body prematurely. This had to be love. As he carried me out of the bathroom and to the bedroom, I thought about Israel. Did I ever feel this way about him? Or were my feelings for him purely based on what I thought he had done for me? Did I still have those feelings for him knowing what I knew now? Could I be with Kimani and be happy with all the memories of our relationship completely erased? My thoughts took a backseat as I felt him dive into me with just enough force to make me inhale sharply.

"Uhhh…"

Tremors shot through my body as he pushed inside me. I had been so lost in my own thoughts that I hadn't even realized he'd come out of his clothes. My eyes shot open, and I realized that he was still dressed from the waist up. Quickly, I helped him out of his shirt, and he hovered his body over mine. Reaching under my body, he grabbed my waist and pulled himself deeper inside of me. I writhed against the sheets as I felt him inching closer and closer to my spot. No words were exchanged because none needed to be. Whatever pain or angst Kimani was going thru, he was transferring that energy to me and I absorbed it immediately, hoping to ease his mind.

"Blu…."

He moaned in my ear before he lightly bit down. Easing his way down my body, he stopped at my breast, taking one nipple into his mouth and aggressively tugging at it. He never lost his rhythm as he drilled into me like he was trying desperately to break me. This wasn't lovemaking; he was fucking me. And I was okay with that. He needed to release whatever it was that he was dealing with, and I wanted to be the one to help him. I was drawn to him. Connected to him in a way that I couldn't describe or remember but I had this urge to be there for him in whatever capacity he needed, and right now he needed a nut. Wrapping my legs around his waist, I pulled him even deeper inside me, and we both let out moans simultaneously. He was hitting my spot so good and so hard that my nails dug into his back like I was trying to escape.

"Fuck, Mani..."

I paused because that came out of nowhere. I knew him as Kimani but calling him by a pet name came with ease. He stopped his stroke for a second when he heard me call him that, but it seemed like it made him go harder. Kimani took my legs, pulled them up in the air and crossed them before he let my ankles rest on his chest. Grabbing at my hips, he plowed into me until he was balls deep and then he went off. He started fucking me at ferocious speeds, and it was feeling so good that I couldn't even bring myself to scream out. I grabbed ahold of his wrist and held on for dear life as he banged my back out.

"'Fuccckkkkkk...." He groaned.

I could feel him shooting his seeds inside me as his body tensed up underneath my grasp. I had come once already, so I was good, plus this wasn't about me. His body language told me that he was dealing with something heavy, and I felt obligated to be there for him. Collapsing next to me, Kimani's chest rose and fell until his breathing was back to normal. I wasn't sure if I should've cuddle with him or give him his space, so I got up from the bed to take care of my hygiene. But, before I got too far, he pulled me back down to the bed. Wrapping his arms around me, I landed on his chest, close to his heart.

"Just lay with me, ma," he said, breathing heavily. We laid there in silence until we both drifted off to sleep.

Grey
August 2015

"Where is her fuckin' doctor at?" I yelled at the nurses behind the station. "I've been standing here for 20 minutes and ain't nobody told me what the hell is going on!"

I was beyond stressed, and the fact that I had no information on my fiancé had me ready to draw blood. Anyone would do, so if these people knew like I knew, they would get someone to me with some information and fast. The nurses behind the station looked scared as hell, and I'm sure the mug on my face didn't help. If a doctor didn't come to tell me what was going on, they had more than my threats to worry about. I stood around for another three minutes or so before a tall white lady, with ice blue eyes and long blond hair approached me with concern on her face. I braced myself for the bad news.

"Kendrick Summers?" she asked, looking down at the tablet in front of her.

"Yeah. What's going on? Where is my fiancé?"

"We had to take her in for emergency surgery. The bullet entered her chest and became lodged in the right ventricle of her heart. We immediately took her into surgery to remove the bullet but during the surgery, she went into shock and slipped into a coma. The next 24 hours are going to be crucial..."

The doctor's voice faded away as I struggled to control my body. Emotions engulfed me like flames, and my whole body threatened to go weak. The words that the doctor was hurling at me lit me up like cop killers straight to the heart; I was dying a quick death. Blaze was the one thing that had kept me centered and focused when everything else had gone to shit. She was my rock, my heart, my future, and without her, there was no way in hell I was going to survive. Pulling myself together, I interrupted the doctor's medical spill.

"Look, I need you to take care of her. Whatever you need, money is no object. I want the best doctors working on her around the clock and---"

"Mr. Summers, I understand you wanting to help, trust me I do. But right now, this isn't about throwing money. This is all up to Blaze. She has to have the will to live in order to get past this critical time. After today, if she makes it through, then we can talk about her medical care moving forward. Until then, I suggest you do the only thing that you can do at the time: Pray."

With that, she placed a sympathetic hand on my shoulder and turned and walked back down the long white corridor. I had the urge to roar and scream out all of the pain that I was feeling, but it was no use. That shit wasn't going to make me feel any better about the situation and it damn sure wasn't going to help Blaze or get me any more answers. I needed to get out of the hospital before I lost my goddamn mind. I started towards the door and was stopped by the nurse.

"Sir! Did you want me to take you down to her room? Visiting hours are over, but I can bend the rules if you want to sneak in for a few moments."

Now this bitch wanted to do her damn job. Calming myself before I hurt her feelings, I shook my head. "No. I'm good."

The nurse looked at me confused probably wondering why after all the drama that I had just put them through I didn't even want to see my fiancé. Truth was, I couldn't take seeing her like that. With tubes and shit running through her body, lifeless and immobile; it was going to break my fucking heart. I just needed to do what I had to do to catch the muthafuckas that did this to her. Like the doc said, the next twenty-four were up to Blaze. I just really hoped that our future was enough of an incentive for her to pull through.

"Well, there were two detectives that stopped by before you arrived. They left their cards. Do you at least want that?" she asked, mild disgust lacing her voice.

"Yeah, man. Give it to me," I requested, unable to contain the annoyance that seeped out.

I was ready to get the fuck out of the hospital, and I definitely wasn't trying to talk to the same muthafuckas that I had spoken to at the crib. I had shit to do, and I needed to act quickly. Time was of the essence, and I needed to get to those bastards before they tried to leave town or before the fucking police tried to piece together everything that happened. Yeah, sure they'd missed me, their intended target, but they for damn sure knew that I was going to be coming after them with a vengeance. If they were smart, they would lay low before trying to come for me again. I was praying that the opposite was true. The nurse handed me a white business card and without even looking at it, I shoved it in my pocket and kept it moving.

As I walked out of the emergency room to the parking lot, guilt damn near swallowed me whole. I knew I was wrong for not at least visiting B, but I couldn't handle it. It was selfish as fuck because I knew that if the tables were turned, she wouldn't even think about leaving my side until my eyes opened. But I didn't want to be sitting in a hospital feeling useless. I needed to be out here, combing the streets and trying to find them fucking pussy ass bitches before the police got ahold of them or worse, the law did. They were mine, and I had no plans of letting anyone get in the way of me finding them.

I slid into my car, stuck the key in the ignition and cranked up the engine. I listened to it purr softly as tears formed pools in my eyes. My phone buzzed in my pocket, and weakly, I reached inside and pulled it out. I hit decline when Nine's name displayed on the screen. I was in no mood to talk with anyone so I would get up with her later. Right now I needed to get home, get some fuckin' sleep and make some moves to find Roman's bitch ass. But before I could even allow myself to pull off, I bowed my head and shot a quick one upstairs:

"God, I know it's been a minute. And if this is Your way of punishing a nigga for not saying his daily prayers...then, man, You cold blooded. But look, that girl in there fighting for her life, she's special to me. An angel like her is probably missed up in heaven but I ain't ready to let You have her back yet, G. I need her here. I need to see her face every day that I wake up and see her smile when she enters the room, or I swear You're going to see me a lot sooner than You anticipated. That's assuming that thugs like me actually make it to heaven. On some real shit, I don't even think I realized what my purpose was until she came into my life. I ain't never had someone love me, man. Ain't a bitch out here that's done for me what she has, and she can't go yet, Man. She CANT! She makes me a better me and I refuse to believe that You put her in my life just to take her away like this. If it's about my lifestyle, I swear this don't mean shit. On everything, I will give up all this, the slanging, the money, the hustling if You bring her back to me. Just do me this one solid. I love her. Please."

I hadn't even realized that the tears had started to roll until the warm, salty liquid landed on my tongue as I spoke. This girl really had a piece of me, and I had to have faith that God was going to look out for a nigga. With my peace being said, I put the car in reverse and pulled out, making my way to the house that was no longer a home.

Blaze
August 2015

Why couldn't I just wake up! I was doing everything in my power to open my eyes or move a finger, but nothing seemed to be happening. I could hear nurses and doctors entering and exiting my room, but they were talking amongst themselves, not to me. The incessant beeping of the machines I was sure that I was hooked up too sounded a little like elevator music to me now that I had listened to them for so long. I wanted nothing more than to turn them suckas off! Outside of the beeps, there was no noise. No one shuffling about and I couldn't sense another presence in the room. Where was Grey?

The beeps grew louder, and I knew it was because of my immediate worry once I realized that Grey was not there with me. Was he ok? Had he been hurt? Or worse taken in by the police? Oh, fuck this. I need to get to my baby.

Determined to wake up, I tried using the muscles in my face to open my eyelids. I strained and strained, but nothing happened. I wanted to scream out my frustration, but no sounds came out. I was stuck inside my shell of a body and even if I tried with everything inside of me, nothing was happening to change that.

I needed to wake up. There was so much that was unsaid before I got shot. I had information for Grey that probably had something to do with the reason somebody went all Wild Wild West in front of his house. The things that I had found out would probably send Grey's world into a tailspin, but without him knowing what I had found out, I knew that whatever he was up to in order to catch the people involved in the shooting, he would be doing it blindly. Silently, I willed my prayer of safety to reach God so that he could protect my baby. Lord knows there were some people after him that were clearly reckless, and I knew that if Grey wasn't hurt or in jail, he was about to become just as wild as they were behind my shooting. If he wasn't in the same predicament that I was in, he was probably on the streets, looking for the people responsible for this. I just hoped that I would be alive to thank him. See, I knew my man and if---

"Long time, no see Cadence."

That voice sent a cold chill down my spine, and my heart exploded. I could hear the beeps getting louder and louder, the speed in which they came increased rapidly. My body jerked violently, and I seized from the sound of him. Soon, I heard the frantic voices of my nurses and doctors, yelling and screaming at each other as they tried desperately to contain the seizure and get my body back to normal. I was scared shitless. Fucking around with Roman, he'd found me. There was no telling what he would do now that he knew where I was. What's that saying? When it rains....

Grey
August 2015

My eyes barely stayed open on the drive home. At least I knew that the man upstairs was still looking out for a nigga because I made it home okay. I was more than exhausted so I dragged myself out of the car and into my house, pausing at the foyer. Flashbacks of the shootout that may end up costing Blaze's life hit me with the force of a Mack Truck, and it took everything in a nigga not to crumble. The thought of losing my baby was too great, so I forced myself to believe that shit was going to work out. Swallowing the emotion that started building up inside me, I closed the door behind me and walked up the stairs after keying in the code to my alarm.

Once upstairs I turned on the shower and stripped out of my clothes. I balled my dreads up into a bun thing on top of my head and stepped underneath the jetted streams of water that came from four different directions inside the custom built masterpiece. The heat and power of the water soothed my aching body, but there was nothing but vengeance and a miracle from God that could ease my mind. I had been totally blindsided by Roman. It had been damn near five years since the shit with Jorge had gone down, and this nigga was just now getting at me? What had taken so long and why now? Was he after something more than revenge? These were questions that were swimming around in my head, but I would be lying if I said I really cared about the answers. All I wanted was that muthafucka's head on a platter.

After about 40 minutes underneath the hot ass water, I stepped out, dried myself off and threw on a pair of gray sweatpants and white t-shirt. As tired as I was, I knew that it was going to be all bad if I didn't put something on my stomach, so I walked downstairs to see what I had in the fridge. As soon as I poked my head inside the refrigerator, a series of loud ass knocks almost made me hit my head on one of the shelves inside. Backing out, I closed the fridge and headed to the door, wondering who the fuck would be outside at 1am. Before I reached the door, I grabbed the 9mm I had tucked under the foyer table. Cocking it back, I aimed it at the door before I swung it open. I didn't have time to fucking play with niggas today.

"What the fuck! Nigga put that shit down!" the female standing outside the door screeched.

My eyebrow rose at the same time my gun did. I didn't know this bitch so I damn sure wasn't letting my guard or gun down before she explained herself. I looked her up and down and frowned after taking a mental inventory. Dressed in a neon yellow spandex dress that did little to cover up her assets and a pair of heels that laced up her boney legs, I knew she was working them streets. On her head sat a cheap blond wig and her make-up looked as though it had been done in the fucking dark.

"So you just gon keep that thang pointed at me?" she asked, loudly chomping away on the piece of gum in her mouth.

"Who are you and why the fuck are you at my door?"

"I can see what she sees in you. You fine as shit! Goddamn!" Her eyes raped me.

"Yo, you got two seconds before I let off rounds. The fuck you want?"

"I'm Porsha, Cadence's sister."

"Man, who the fuck is Cadence? I don't know any Cadence."

She rolled her green eyes which I automatically assumed were contacts. Turning around and leaning to the side, she motioned for someone to come from around the bush. I aimed directly at that muthafucka because I didn't know what the fuck this rabid looking bitch had up her sleeve. A few seconds later, a pretty little girl, no more than about eight years old, came walking out, eyes big as saucers as she took a look at the gun I had aimed at her. Porsha turned around to me.

"Oh my God! Put that shit down! Damn! You gon shoot a little girl?"

"You better get to talking bitch." I seethed.

"Like I said, I'm Porsha, Cadence's sister. But you know her as Blaze. I don't know where the fuck she got that name from or why that would be her choice pick for her new government but whatever. Anyway this---"

"Wait, wait, wait. Who the fuck are you talking about?" I was lost. I heard what the fuck she said, but she wasn't making sense to me.

"Damn, for someone who is supposed to be 'the man' round here, you sure are fucking slow! Let me spell it out for you, dummy. Your bougie ass, high-class, wanna-be fiancé, Blaze, ain't shit but a pump faker. She's really just her daddy's down ass bitch and the mother of this here sister-daughter."

"Bitch, what? You talking in riddles. You know what? Fuck this. Get off my property before I call the *cleaners* to come get you."

Lowering my gun, I turned around and walked inside the house, shutting the door. I had enough of the bullshit! This night had been one from the deepest pits of hell, and I just wanted it to be over. So I decided to take my ass to bed, foregoing the food altogether. I set the alarm again, turned off the lights and headed upstairs. As soon as my body touched the soft, pillow top mattress, a nigga was out like a light.

- -

The next morning, I woke up feeling rested but still bogged down with all the shit on my mind. I had a lot of shit to accomplish today, and I promised myself that I was going to get over to the hospital today and see my lady like I should have done last night. My stomach growled as soon as my feet hit the floor, sounding like an African drum. *Cadence.* That shit that ol' girl was popping last night suddenly resurfaced in my mind. She was talking in circles, but from what I could put together, she was trying to tell me that she was Blaze's sister, whose real name wasn't actually Blaze but Cadence, and that she had fucked her dad and had a sister, I mean, daughter. The shit blew me, and I felt like maybe I shouldn't read into it too much because Porsha could've been on that shit.

Shaking the thoughts out of my head, I stepped into the bathroom to wash my face and brush my teeth before I ventured downstairs to get some food. Once I reached the bottom of the stairs, a shadow at the door caught my attention. Slowly, I made my way over to the table to grab my gun. This shit was never going to end, huh? Well, fuck it. Whoever was outside was getting one to the dome, no questions asked. Swinging the door open wildly, I pointed my piece in the direction of the shadow.

"The fuck?" I mumbled, blinking a few times to make sure that what I was seeing was real.

Cuddled up in the corner of my porch was the little girl from last night. She had her knees to her chest and a small, stuffed animal sticking out from underneath her arm. Her eyes grew as she stared down the barrel of the gun, but I was too shocked to move a muscle.

"I didn't do anything," she whispered, tucking her head under her arm in fear.

Finally, I snapped out of it and lowered the gun, stuffing it in the waistband of my sweatpants. Kneeling down beside her, I tapped her arm and her head slowly moved until her eyes met mine.

"You been out here all night?" I asked. She nodded her head. "What's your name, sweetie?"

"Harmony," she all but whispered.

I extended my hand. "My name is Kendrick. But my friends call me Grey."

Baby girl looked at it, and slowly a smile stretched across her face. A small giggle shot out of her little body, and it was contagious. I laughed and then held my hand to my chest in mock offense.

"Why you laughing at me? You don't want to be my friend? Dang, that's messed up."

Continuing my charade, I stood up and poked my lips out like I was upset. A few seconds later, I felt a small tug at my pants. I looked down, and Harmony was staring up at me smiling.

"I was laughing at your name. Grey is a color not a name," she said, smiling.

"Dang! You don't want to be my friend *and* you clowning my name! You hurt my feelings, girl. See, I was going to take you to get some big ol' pancakes with a bunch of toppings and whipped cream on em' but since you wanna be a bully..." I started to walk back in the door, and I could hear her scurrying to get up.

"Wait...I'll be your friend."

I turned around and smiled at her, folding my arms across my chest.

"Oh, *now* you wanna be my friend because I mentioned pancakes?" She giggled. "You are something else, Harmony. But because I really want you to be my friend, I'ma let you come inside and wait for me to get dressed then we can go get pancakes, ok?"

Harmony smiled wide as she nodded her head. Moving to the side, I let her walk over the threshold before peeking back out to make sure there was no one else outside. Shaking my head, I closed the door behind me and had Harmony follow me into the living room. Picking up the remote, I handed it to Harmony who had made herself comfortable on the couch.

"I don't know what channel the cartoon station is but---"

"I know the station," she said as she switched on the TV.

Throwing my hands up in the air, I stepped aside and let her do her thang. I watched her for a few moments before leaving the room and walking upstairs to my bedroom. Sitting on the edge of my bed, I buried my head in my hands, willing this fucking nightmare to disappear. Not only was my fiancé in the hospital fighting for her life, but I had two bitter mutherfuckas after me, my brother's snitching ass was what brought us here, my fiancé may not be who she said she was and a child that may or may not be her sister or daughter was just dropped off at my doorstep. What the fuck else could happen?

Blu
August 2015

When I woke up the next morning, Kimani was already gone. I was a little disappointed that he jetted because although the connection that we obviously shared was still strong, I felt the need to get to know him all over again. Plus, my living arrangements and our future hadn't been discussed, and I felt a little out of place here at his home. Not to mention I only had the money I'd taken from Israel, which didn't amount to shit, so I wasn't sure what I was going to do.

Sighing, I swung my legs over the edge of the bed and stood. Stark naked, I walked out of the bedroom, through the hallway and to the kitchen to grab a bottle of water. I jumped out of my skin when I saw a tall, well-dressed man sitting cross-legged on the couch, texting away. He looked up just as I tried to cover myself and he laughed out loud.

He waved his hand delicately in my direction. "Oh, honey, trust me; I don't want none of what you got over there."

"I…uhhh…wait just a minute."

Even though he was as feminine as I was, I still wasn't comfortable with him seeing all my goodies. So I hurried back to the bedroom and threw on a fresh pair of underwear and a knit sweat suit and sauntered back into the kitchen.

"Okay, so now who are you?" I asked him bluntly.

"Marques Julani, stylist to the stars, hunny. You're Blu, I presume?" He extended his hand for me to shake.

"I am. But why…"

"Mr. Kimani hired me to get you together. Just between you and me, he spared no expense when it came to you because honey, I am not cheap especially not on short notice."

He switched out the room leaving me hella confused. When he came back, he was wheeling two large carts filled with clothes, shoes, handbags and accessories. I was floored.

"This…this is for me?"

"Yes, girl. I got a little bit of everything. From Target and Marshall's to TopShop and Jimmy Choo. If you a label whore, we gon' have some issues." He looked me up and down anticipating my response.

"Please, I live in Target, Marshall's and anything in between. Ain't no shame in my fashion game." I chuckled.

"Yasss! I love it! Okay, let's get started. By the way, we have a friend of mine, Tatum, coming over to whip your hair in an hour or two, kay?"

Without giving me a chance to respond, he pulled at my hand and dragged me over to the racks of clothes he had pulled for me. He wasn't lying when he said he had a little bit of everything. I tried on outfit after outfit, only stopping for a few swigs of water. After two hours, I decided to keep everything that he had brought. I was really digging Marques' personality and was glad to have a little bit of entertainment while Kimani was gone. I was just about to ask him if he wanted to go get drinks later on when the doorbell rang. Assuming it was his friend Tatum, I let him answer it while I used the bathroom. A few minutes later I came into the room to find Marques foaming at the mouth over a tall, vanilla latte colored man with sandy brown dreads. He was gorgeous and was holding a pretty little girl's hand.

"Hi," I spoke and all eyes turned on me.

"Hey, Blu. You remember me?"

My heart skipped a few beats and a light film of sweat formed on my forehead. I was hoping that he wasn't someone else I needed to run from.

"No, should I?"

"Uh, I'm Grey, Kimani's brother. I used to date…um…"

A light bulb went off, and I remembered Kimani telling me about his brother that used to date Nakami.

"My best friend, Nakami," I said finishing his sentence. "You're the one they're after."

"Apparently. Look, do you mind if we talk privately for a second?" He scratched his head and then shoved his unoccupied hand down into his pocket.

"Yeah, sure."

Grey kneeled down in front of the little girl and smiled.

"Harmony, I'm going to have a talk with my friend for a minute. Just sit out here until I come back ok?"

"Okay," she responded shyly.

Marques looked at me with wide eyes and then at Harmony. He read my expression and threw his hands up in the air.

"What? I was an only child. I don't know what to do with this!" he exclaimed.

"Just let her watch some cartoons or something, man," Grey threw over his shoulder.

We walked into Kimani's bedroom, and Grey shut the door behind him. He leaned against the door and sighed heavily. He was an extremely attractive man and the first man with dreads I had ever considered pretty, but the stress of what he was going through was written all over his face. He looked tired and worn down, and I could empathize with his pain. I sat on the corner of the bed waiting for him to say something. It took him a few minutes, but he finally spoke.

"I'm glad you back home, B. My brother was going through it thinking you were..." his voice trailed off.

"Thanks."

It was awkward, this exchange, because I had to be told what had happened and while I could feel that Grey was truly sorry for what had happened to me, there was a disconnect because I didn't remember him at all.

"But look, I need some information from you. You know the people that are after me better than I do and I need to get to them before they get to me."

Nervously, I wrung my hands. Sure, Grey deserved to know what Israel had been planning with his brother, but I felt this weird allegiance to him. Don't get me wrong; he was a fuck boy for sure for all the things he'd done to me in order to get to Grey. But at one point I swore I was in love with him, and some of those feelings still lingered. Grey sensed my hesitation and ran his hands down the sides of his face in irritation.

"Blu, I like you. I really do. And I think that you're good for my brother, but if you are still working with them bitch ass niggas I will shoot you where you stand and sing a hymn at your funeral like I'm none the wiser."

I didn't take offense to his statement because I knew he had every reason to be upset and looking for answers. His fiancé had been shot as a result of the beef Israel had with him, and I felt partially responsible even though I didn't have a clue what was going on and who his intended target was.

"I'm not sure what I can tell you. He didn't tell me the plan. He was just...just...I don't know. Training me or something."

"C'mon B, think. I know you know more than that. Where did they rest their heads, names of friends or associates that they came across, businesses that they frequented? I need more than that lil' bullshit you just spit."

I sighed. I could understand his frustration, but I really didn't know shit.

"We lived in Atlanta mostly. We moved here about a month ago and were living in the condo that Kimani went to. I think that they own the building," I finally admitted.

"Good, now we getting somewhere. Let me have the address."

He handed me his phone which he had opened up to the notes app, and I typed in the address of the building where I used to live with Israel. I was hoping that this was enough to get Grey a lead and off my back because I didn't think that I could help him with any more information. I handed him his phone back and stood to exit the room, but Grey grabbed my arm, making me turn towards him.

"Like I said before, I like you, Blu. But if you're bullshitting me in any way, shape or form or if you hurt my brother, it'll be nothing to make death your reality. Long as you do right by me and my brother, I'll consider you family but the minute I think that I can't trust you—"

"I got it."

Grey nodded his head and let go of my arm. I brushed past him and into the hallway with him right behind me. We entered the living room to see Marques and the little girl he'd called Harmony, playing dress up in the clothes that Marques had brought over. I watched them dance around the living room with a smirk on my face.

"Oh, I forgot to ask you. Could you watch her for a couple hours?" Grey whispered.

"Seriously? You threaten my life because you aren't sure that you trust me and then ask if you can leave a child in my care? You're missing a few screws."

"So they tell me," he laughed. "So is that a yes?"

I rolled my eyes, and he laughed. Stepping further into the room, we grabbed Marques and Harmony's attention, and they turned to us in a fit of laughter. Grey walked over to Harmony and explained that he would be leaving for a little while and asked if she would be okay chilling with me and Marques. She looked over at me for reassurance, and I nodded my head at her and gave her a thumbs up. Grey handed her a few hundred dollar bills, chucked the deuces and left.

Israel
August 2015

I looked down at my buzzing phone and gritted my teeth. I was tired of Roman calling me every two seconds, but I knew that if I didn't answer soon, he would keep trying his hand. Irritated that I had to adjust my focus, I brought the phone up to my ear and answered.

"What nigga, damn!"

"Bout time you answered! Where the fuck you at, yo?"

"Minding my business. What do you want? I told you I was done with your shit show."

I watched Grey exit the house where Blu was staying, and instead of concentrating on him, I tried to look past him, praying to get just the tiniest glimpse of the woman that had stolen my heart. The door slammed firmly behind him and to say that I was disappointed would be an understatement. I just wanted to see her, but I was a little nervous about how she would react to seeing me in person. So I had started following her. Unbeknownst to her, there was a tracking chip in the watch that she wore, so even though she thought she had gotten away from me, I could still find her.

"Are you even fucking listening to me?" Roman roared through the phone.

"No! That's the whole damn point. I'm done listening and taking orders from you. You want Grey; you go get him. I'm good. You just fucking shit up for the rest of us."

"Oh, I get it. I knew I shouldn't have let your weak ass around some pussy."

My nostrils flared at his implication.

"Says the nigga that fucked his apprentice. Get the fuck outta here. Look, it ain't nothing you can do or say to get me back in the fold. I got other shit I need to get done and you holding me up trying to avenge a death that I'm sure pops saw coming. I'm here for you because you're my brother, but don't hit my line with this silly bullshit no more. "

I ended the call and tossed my phone back into the cup holder it had been resting in. I left out a few breaths, trying to calm myself down. I understood Roman's anger. I wished that my pops was still alive, but the truth of the matter was that he wasn't, and there wasn't anything that was going to bring him back. So all this plotting and planning was over the top to me, and I didn't have time for it. I never wanted to follow in my father's footsteps anyway, so the fall of his empire was a Godsend in a way. Roman, on the other hand, I believed wanted to be a carbon copy of our father. He wouldn't admit it, but I didn't need him to in order for me to believe that it was true. Truth was, I wasn't sure what I wanted to do with my life outside of the family business, but I couldn't focus on figuring that out right now. My mind was on one thing and one thing only. Blu.

Grey had hopped in his car and sped off, and I was stuck staring at the boss ass house that Blu was currently chilling in. Her old nigga was a fucking male model of all things and apparently his career was able to afford him some nice digs…and my bitch. I couldn't understand why after all that I had done for her, she would go running back to a nigga that she didn't even halfway remember. I knew she couldn't remember much about him because I had made sure that she couldn't. Fucking up her memory had been the only thing that I had been able to convince my brother to agree to, and he only agreed because it also benefited him in the long run. I thought that it would guarantee that Blu would always be mine, but I had underestimated the love that she thought she had lost.

But there would be no more fuck ups on my end. I was going to show her that I was the one that deserved to love her for the rest of her life, not that lil' pansy ass nigga that made his living making duck lips for the camera. I wasn't going to approach her now, but once I had a plan together, I was going to get my girl back, and I was never letting her go.

Karma
August 2015

"What the fuck do you mean he's not here?" I asked.

My voice had reached a pitch that only dogs could hear.

"Ma'am, I'm going to need you to calm down," the nurse behind the desk stated sternly.

"I'll calm down once you tell me where the fuck my fiancé is!"

These bitches were either retarded or deaf because they acted like I was speaking a different language. I know for a fact that a nigga got hit with a slug last night and with this being the closest hospital to Grey's house, this is where he should be. These bumbling, community college-degree-having ass hoes needed to cough up some information quickly before it turned into John Q in this bitch.

"Are ya'll stupid or something? He came from 26154 Dix street! Find him before I knock on every door in this bitch!"

The nurse eyed me with annoyance, and I rolled my eyes. It was clear I wasn't getting anywhere with this bitch without giving her some motivation. I reached in my purse and pulled out three one hundred dollar bills. Folding them up into my hand, I slid them across the desk nonchalantly. She took the bills and stuffed them in her pocket quickly while looking around to see if anyone had noticed the exchange. Confident that she hadn't been caught, the nurse typed something into the computer and then looked at me with a raised eyebrow.

"What?"

"There was no Kendrick Summers that was admitted like I said previously, but there was a victim from that address who was brought here."

"Who?"

"A Blaze McGowen."

Blaze? She was the one that was hit? Shit! That meant that Grey was out turning the city of Los Angeles upside down to try and find out who was behind things. That was going to make it harder for me to get to him because he was going to be bouncing from city to city to get answers and his moves would be more unpredictable than they already were. I could only assume that he would come here to visit Blaze, but there was little that I could do to him while we were in the hospital. Too many muthafuckas in and out and cameras were in every corner of this place.

"What room is she in?"

The nurse looked at me hesitantly, like she wasn't sure if she should give me the room number. What the fuck was I going to do in a hospital full of muh'fuckas in the middle of the day?

"Uh...hello?" I snapped my fingers in front of her face.

"Room 1212."

I stalked off without another word and followed the signs that led to Blaze's room. I entered cautiously, hoping that there wasn't anyone else in the room. I wasn't ready to reveal myself just yet seeing how everyone thought I was dead, and it was easier for me to move around if everyone still thought that. Upon entering the room, I noticed that she had been put up in a swanky private room. The shit smelled like lavender and honey as opposed to the sterile and stale smell the rest of the hospital carried and she had a flat screen TV that was playing cable. The fuck she need cable for, I wondered. Looking at her, she looked dead. Peering outside her room, I checked to make sure no one was coming before I grabbed the chart that hung on her door. Flipping through it, I was able to gather that she had survived a bullet to the chest only to fall into a coma during her surgery.

"Hmph. That's what you get, you overweight, man-stealing whore," I hissed.

I hung the file back on her door and pinned my arms against my chest. My brain was starting to work in overdrive as a plan began to develop beautifully. Slowly, I strutted over to the bed where Blaze lay unconscious and bent down so that my mouth was eye level to her ear.

"I'm coming back for you, missy. You're going to help me get Grey back where he belongs."

Kimani
September 2015

Stressed wasn't a strong enough word to explain how I was feeling. I had laid all my sins in front of my brother, and he had reacted just the way that I expected him too. My secret had been made worse by the predicament it had landed my brother and his fiancé in and I felt like the weight of it all had fallen on me. So I felt obligated to help sort all this shit out and find the niggas that had thrown our worlds into a tailspin. From what Blu told me, their names were Roman and Israel, and they were the sons of Jorge Nueva, our old drug connect and they were out for blood. I can't even front and say that I knew where to start to find these niggas, but I was determined. The first place that I went was to that address that Dustin had given me on Blu. She had stated that she had been living there for a while, and I thought that was as good a place as any to try and get some answers.

I walked into the building and was greeted by the same mousy white nigga that had been there the first time. He looked up from his computer and smiled wide, prepared to go into the long spiel of a greeting that he was required to give. I cut him off with a wave of my hand.

"The owners. Where are they?"

"Excuse me?"

"Man, you heard me. The owners of the building…where are they at? I need to speak with them."

He fumbled around with the phone on the desk, nervousness apparent in his eyes.

"May I ask why you would like to speak with the owners?"

"You can ask, but that don't mean that I'm going to tell you. Just get them out here."

My upper lip curled towards my nose due to my annoyance. Ol' boy nodded his head and started making his call. I turned my back to him and placed my hands in my pockets. My phone buzz against my hands, and I pulled it out and looked at the caller ID. It was my manager Steph. This was the sixth call from her that I had dodged today. With attitude, I hit accept and raised the phone up to my ear.

"Yes?" I answered tightly.

"Where the hell have you been, Kimani! I've been calling you all morning!" she screamed.

"Yo, stop all that damn screaming. I saw your calls, but I've been busy. Handling some family stuff. What do you need?"

"What do I..." she paused, and I could hear her sucking in a breath before she continued. "What I *needed* was for you to have been on set three hours ago. Shooting of season two started yesterday, Kimani!"

"Shit!"

"Yeah, 'shit' is right. I understand your family stuff. It was all over the news today. And while I'm sure things are heavy in your personal life, with headlines like the ones that were all over everywhere last night and this morning, your professional life is about to get heavy as well. I have TMZ and E News calling me every ten minutes looking for an official statement and the reality producer is up my ass because you missed your call time."

I paced the floor with steam shooting from my ears. Now was not the time for this bullshit!

"Steph, look..."

She cut me off before I could get started good.

"Make your way to 91588 Sunset now or so help me God..."

"Aight, Steph. Damn."

I hung up on her before I was subjected to any more of her mouth and let a small groan. I could definitely feel a headache coming on.

"Sir?"

I turned around to face the receptionist or whatever that nigga was and wrinkles knotted across my forehead. There were two European-looking dudes in expensive suits standing next to him, hands in their pocket trying their hardest to place my face.

"Who are they?" I asked.

"The owners. Preston Kilani and Trenton Stefanopolus."

"No. No, no. These are not the owners."

The man with the thin mustache chuckled before turning to me.

"Not that I need to explain anything to you, but we purchased this building two days ago from a dear friend."

"A dear friend by the name of Roman Nueva?" I sneered.

The other man looked down at his watch and looked up at me smiling.

"Good luck on your search of this Roman Nueva that you are inquiring about. But with a newly acquired building comes meetings upon meetings and it looks as if we are running late for the first one of the day. "

Without another word, they turned and walked towards the elevator. I wanted to show my ass and let them know that my brother and I were not to be played with, but before I could summon up enough energy to do so, I heard a loud commotion behind me.

"What the…"

I turned to face the glass door behind me, and a barrage of people with cameras stood there, snapping pictures of a nigga and shooting questions like bullets.

"Is Grey Summers ok?"

"Do you know who was behind the shooting?"

"Will this be on the next season of Almost Famous?"

"How will this affect your career going forward?"

"Was this drug-related?"

I just stood there stuck like I had gotten my foot trapped in quicksand, and stared at them. Sure, I'd had run-ins with the paparazzi before but never to this extent. It was usually one or two of them, and it was normally arranged by Steph to get me a little publicity, but this was crazy. How had they even known where I was? How the fuck was I going to find anything out about what happened with cameras and shit following my every move and Steph up my ass? Fuck! I was screwed. I guess the reception guy saw that I was about to flip out, and he quickly stepped up.

"Sir, I can take you down to the basement and have you go out the underground parking exit if you'd like."

"Yeah, man. Get me the fuck outta here."

Ol' boy nodded his head and motioned for me to follow him. We traveled down a couple flights of stairs before we hit the dark and dusty parking garage. I extended my hand to him, grateful that he was able to get me away from that madness. Now I just had to get to my car without alerting the paparazzi.

"Thanks, man. And if you have any more information on the real owners of the building give me a call."

I pulled out a card from my wallet and handed it to him. He accepted it and my handshake.

"I'm willing to pay for valuable information. Information that you keep to yourself and don't give to the police when they stop by."

I looked him square in the eye to make sure that he caught my drift. He nodded his head and walked away. I took a deep breath and blew out the air harshly. My life was about to become a shit show. I could feel it.

Grey
September 2015

After dropping the kid off with Blu, I went to meet up with Brandin and Cope at After Midnight. I hoped that they had more information that could help me find these sucka ass niggas and quickly because I felt like shit for not being there for Blaze. I knew that there was a definite timetable on getting at Roman and his brother before they either went in hiding or struck again, so I just had to hope that my prayer had reached God and that he would keep Blaze safe and recovering in the meantime.

I hopped out of my car and headed into After Midnight with a scowl on my face. Stressed wasn't even the word for how I felt and even though I enjoyed being in the presence of my closet niggas, today wasn't a social call by far. I walked inside the building and headed to the bar where Brandin and Cope were sitting, already a drink in. They both turned in my direction when they felt my presence. I had known B the longest. Brandin was the color of patent leather, but the ladies loved his dark ass. He kept his hair cut low with a thick chin strap beard that was always crispy as fuck. This nigga thought he was a part time model or some shit so he was always dressed like he ran in them fashion circles or something.

Cope was a little weird looking ass nigga that we always joked on. He wasn't weird looking for real, but he was my complexion with red ass hair everywhere. I don't know how his mixed ass had come out looking like the Brawny lumberjack, but the shit was comical to me. He was hood as hell though and one of the most thorough niggas on my team. He was a hitta and he could body a nigga with little to no effort and make them disappear like magic. If ever there were two niggas that could help me get to Roman, it was these two. I walked up on them and dapped them up.

"What up, bro?" I asked Brandin before I took a seat at the bar.

After Midnight wasn't open but I had called the bartender in to tend to us and was paying her for the whole day. A nigga needed a well-poured drink like a muthafucka.

"Shit, man."

"Ya'll got something for me?"

Cope slid a folder across the bar towards me before he started talking.

"These niggas is wild, B. Especially this nigga Israel. Nigga been locked up plenty. His rap sheet long as fuck.

They owned that building that matches with the address you gave me, but it looks like it was sold a few days ago."

I thumbed through the folder as Brandin jumped into the conversation.

"They own a couple retail stores in Atlanta. Nothing major, just some sneakers and shit but no businesses anywhere else. They don't have any deeds in their name nor do they have any leases out under their social, so we can't be sure where they are laying their head."

"They do have a sister, though. She's at the U of M hospital in a vegetative state. Her name is Italia."

"Shit..." I mumbled.

It was no wonder these niggas were coming after me. If I thought some niggas had caused this much destruction in my life, I would be gunning for them too. But now that they had made their move, and my fiancé was laying in the hospital fighting for her life, I had no sympathy for them, niggas. I'm sure Italia didn't have shit to do with anything, and that was fucked up but neither did Blaze.

"I guess that's where I'll start then. I know some people in the D that can help me get some more information. Anything else?"

I looked up from the file and could see that Brandin and Cope were both apprehensive about something. They looked at each other and clammed up.

"What the fuck? Spit it out."

Mentally, I braced myself for whatever bullshit they were about to throw at me. I was hoping that they weren't about to tell me that one of them niggas was dead because it was going to kill me to not be able to murder them myself.

"After taking a look at their birth certificates…it looks like ya'll are brothers."

Roman
September 2015

"Let me get the filet mignon with garlic mashed potatoes and sautéed asparagus. What do you want, sweetheart?"

I turned and looked at the beauty that sat on the sofa of my hotel room. She had gotten comfortable, kicking her heels off near the coffee table and tucking her feet underneath her butt. Her head rested on her fist as she looked over the room service menu carefully. She turned to me and smiled.

"Can I have the rosemary chicken with fingerling potatoes and the mixed vegetables? No butter on the veggies, please. Oh and some white wine would be nice."

I nodded and placed her order. I hung up the phone after hearing that the food would be ready in forty minutes. I joined my company on the couch and couldn't help but stare at her. She blushed under gaze. She was definitely beautiful.

"What? What you staring at me like that for?"

"You're beautiful. You know that?"

"I do. But what's your aim here? You don't have to douse me in compliments to get my attention. If you didn't have it, I wouldn't be here." She smirked.

"The compliments weren't anything but compliments. They weren't meant to sway you into helping me. But, cool. I'll get to the point. I need your help getting Kimani."

Vicious looked up at me, her eyes urging me to continue.

"He's caught up in a contract under Stephanie, and he's going to be tied to that reality series for way longer than he wants to be. I've taken a look through his contract with my lawyers and the way things are drawn up, the reality show takes top priority over any other appearances, shows or gigs which in turn can hinder his career."

I snuck a glance at Vicious, and she was eating up my lies like it was a five-star brunch. After racking my brain trying to figure out how I was going to get at Grey without the resources and people that I initially had on my side, I hopped on the internet. I combed through every article that mentioned Kimani or Grey and finally came up with a plan. I would use Kimani to get to Grey. He was the only family that he had so to lose Kimani, even temporarily, would send Grey into a tailspin and I knew that that would lead him back to me.

So I had gotten in touch with Vicious through a friend of a friend and posed as an agent looking to sign Kimani. I knew from the articles that I had read on TMZ and The Shade Room that they had once been an item, and that from the reality show that Kimani had recently shot, she was still trying to win him back. So she was the perfect person to lure him in and bring him to me. She was bait, and she didn't even know it.

"So how am I supposed to help?" she asked.

"Well, you seem to know him best. So I was hoping that you could talk to him for me. Get him to see where I'm coming from."

I paused to let her think it over. She removed her feet from under her body and stood up. Pacing around the room, she ran her hands through her hair, her brain working in overdrive. Suddenly, she stopped.

"Why do you need me, though? If you can offer him something his current agent can't, why would I need to convince him to speak to you?"

"Because I've tried that already. I've even presented him with the contract and showed him the clause that puts his career in jeopardy. But he trusts Stephanie and thinks that I'm just out to get paid. Which, I can't argue with. The major motive is the money, but I honestly pride myself on being an honest businessman. Kimani could be doing big things and his current set up is going to do nothing but hinder his success."

"Ok say that I believe you, which I'm not completely positive that I do. What do I get out of the deal?"

"You get Kimani. After he sees what you have done for him and that you have his best interest at heart, he'll jump at the chance to get you back."

She hit me with a side eye before placing her hand on her curvy hip.

"Boy, please. If I haven't won him over already, this lil' mess ain't hardly going to land me back in his bed. I need something more concrete than that, or you can count me out."

Damn, she was smarter than she thought. There was only one other thing that I knew of that would make Vicious do what I asked, but that would involve me working a whole lot of favors on my end and possibly even taking someone out. But I was fucking desperate at this point. I needed to get Grey before the boys got at me. I was giving myself two weeks to handle business and get the fuck up out of LA. And two weeks was stretching it, but it gave me time to put a plan b in place just in case Vicious didn't come through for me. But after I presented her with the offer, I had no doubt that she would go along with my request.

"Okay, well how about I help you get you the one thing that you want more than Kimani."

Her eyebrow arched.

"And what is that?"

"A career as a solo artist."

Vicious stopped dead in her tracks and faced me with wide eyes. I smiled on the inside knowing that I'd captured her attention. I found out that there was trouble brewing amidst the group members of Wild 1's. Vicious was never interested in being in a girl group to begin with but at the time she auditioned for her record label, her vocals weren't strong enough to jumpstart a solo career. Along the way she'd gained a Rihanna like personality and her vocals had vastly improved. Unfortunately, she was stuck in a tight contract with her label, and there was no way out until her group released three more albums and signed on for two more tours.

"That's impossible. My contract is—"

I cut her off. "Your contract is a non-factor to me, sweetheart. If I want it done, I can make it happen. Get Kimani to meet with me and your dreams will become reality."

She was quiet as she continued to stare at me in disbelief. She was probably finding it hard to believe that I was able to hold up my end of the bargain because numerous people had already looked into her contract, and saw that it was air tight. But I knew that she wasn't stupid. I knew that by now she knew that I wasn't everything that I said I was. And because she knew that, I was sure that she was thinking of the moral implications of fucking with me. I was willing to bet all my money that she was trying to decide whether to sell her soul for her dreams or walk out and save herself now.

"Fine. I'll do it."

Soul sold.

Blu
September 2015

If I stared at the same damn wall for another minute, I was going to lose my fucking mind. I was bored to tears, and again Kimani was nowhere to be found. He had been coming in late and leaving early for the last couple days for early call time on the reality show that he was shooting. I was cool with that. Really, I was. I understood that his career was demanding and that he would be on the go a lot of the time, but I had been cooped up in the house alone since we had found our way back to each other. I was growing frustrated and restless. I wanted to talk and try and sort things out. I needed to re-learn Kimani and get my life back.

The only instructions I had been given from both Kimani and Grey were to stay away from people from my past. I was never told that I couldn't leave the house, but then again, Israel had never told me that I couldn't either. But I was beyond bored. I wasn't used to sitting around like a spiritless housewife waiting for someone to give me permission to jump start my life again. I was a boss bitch who ran her own shit and moved by her own rules. With that final thought, I hopped up off the bed and reached for my cell phone.

"Marques Julani. How can I upgrade you today?"

I puckered my lips. "Hey, this is Blu. Kimani's girl...uh friend," I corrected, unsure of how to define myself when it came to Kimani.

"Hey, Blu's girl. What's up mama?"

"Are you busy tonight? Well, like around 5 or 6?"

"Let me check, baby doll. One second."

When he put me on a brief hold, I stood and stretched my body. I walked around Kimani's bedroom wearing just a pair of boy shorts and a tank top, admiring the modern, masculine way that it was decorated. Kimani was one of the only people that I knew in this day and age that still preferred carpet to wood floors, and he had picked the softest and most luxurious mink carpet. It was deep, dark gray that sunk like quicksand with every step, and was the most heavenly thing I had ever experienced in a home. His walls were painted the same color of his carpet, making the room very sensual and dark. There were framed pictures along the wall behind his bed; all different sizes like in a gallery. There were large, built-in shelves that blended in with the wall and held knickknacks and books to the right of his California king size bed and two leather armchairs sat on the left. The only deviation from the darkness of the room was the rich brown, almost gold lamps that were on his nightstands and the small table in between the leather chairs. All in all, it was beautiful in a very manly type of way.

"Hey, Blu," Marques said, after coming back on the line. "I'm free after six. What's up, girl? You need me to style you for an event?"

"I wish. I was just hoping that you would want to go grab some drinks with me."

"Oh girl, you should have opened with that. Marques is always down for alcohol. You mind if I call Tatum and see if she wants to go? She been texting me about her man problems and I ain't got time to play Dr. Phil by text."

I laughed. "Yeah, I was going to ask if you would invite her anyway. Do you know of a good place to go? You know I really don't know L.A. like that."

"Honey, do I? Let's do The Parlor on Melrose. It's always some eye candy up in there. Not that you need any with both of them fine ass white chocolate men up and through your house. Hmph!"

I burst out laughing at his crazy ass.

"Okay, that sounds good to me. I'll text you when I'm on my way."

"Okay, boo. See you later."

I hung up with Marques excited to get out of the house for a change. It was only two in the afternoon, so I decided to fix myself a quick bite to eat and lay down before I hopped in the shower to get ready for happy hour.

Three hours later, I was hopping out of the shower feeling rejuvenated. I turned on my Teyana Taylor station on Pandora and Alessa Cera's "Here" came floating through the room. I grabbed my tiny bag of products that Israel had given me and headed into the bathroom to do my makeup first. Most of the time that I was with Israel, I didn't wear make-up because he preferred it that way. But in an effort to make up for the constant mood swings and temper tantrums, he had stopped by the MAC counter and asked the sales lady to load me up with some essentials. I made a mental note to ask Kimani about going to the mall to grab a few more things.

"No. No," I said aloud, shaking my head. "No more asking for fucking permission. You are a grown ass woman," I chastised myself in the mirror.

I was over being meek; the shit didn't even feel right. Tonight, I was going to go out and get drinks with my new friend and try for once in the past year to feel normal. Tomorrow I was getting my ass to a mall by myself and doing what I wanted to do instead of waiting around for Kimani to tell me it was okay. I had never needed a man to do anything for me, especially not give me permission to do me, so I was over the shit. I hummed along with Pandora as I applied my make-up. After my face was lightly beat, I untied the scarf around my head and combed down the amazing blowout that Tatum had given me. I had never seen my hair so full and pretty. I had a few bonded pieces in the back for length and after wrapping the wand curls, I had very soft and romantic waves. I was digging it.

Done with hair and make-up, I walked out to the living room where the racks of clothes that Kimani had bought me still stood and I perused through the selection. I settled on a pair of brown suede, high-waisted bell bottom TopShop pants, a cream colored lace crop top, and a pair of nude Gianvitto Rossi pumps. A large pair of hoops and a delicate gold hand chain were my only accessories aside from the Saint Laurent fringe handbag in the same color as my pants. I passed by the large mirror in his foyer and had to admit that looking this good made me feel more like myself. I winked at my reflection before I headed outside to the awaiting Uber.

"You did not come to play with these hoes! You came to slay, bitch! *Yasss!*" Marquis shouted as I walked up the stairs to the open patio area of The Parlor.

I laughed at his crazy ass before giving him a hug. He looked good too but with him being a stylist, I expected nothing less. Behind him Tatum stood with a smile on her face, waiting to give me a hug. I had seen some pretty bitches in my lifetime, but Tatum was so damn gorgeous it was ridiculous. She had this dewy, brownie colored skin tone that even in person looked as if it was photoshopped. She had the cutest little button nose and upturned lips, but it was her pretty, wide grayish brown eyes that made her unique. She had long, straight black hair that flowed over her shoulders and stopped in the middle of her back and there wasn't a track up in the mix. She was a slim chick with big breasts; she was built like that chick India Love. And she was one of the sweetest people you ever wanted to meet. Bypassing Marquis, I reached over to hug Tatum and then sat down at their table.

"Girl, I need to get you to do a photo shoot with me or something. You got that look, honey!" Marquis exclaimed.

"I was just thinking the same thing. I'm going to start making custom wigs, and you would be perfect as the face of the line." Tatum said.

"Whoa, whoa. I'm not a model. I'm just—"

"Uh-uh! That's what you're not going to do in my presence. You are everything and anything you want to be, boo. I know you've been through some things but hell, everybody has. Don't let that shit dull your shine. You have a face and body that was born to make these thot bots jealous. So if you don't use it, I'ma cut your silly ass." Marquis said as he pointed his long, manicured finger in my face.

Tatum and I looked at each other and burst out laughing. This boy was a fool.

"Laugh all you want but a bitch still keeps a razor under the tongue to slice a bitch up like some cold cuts. So you got one more time to come at me with that modest bullshit before I go Lucy Lui on that ass!" He rolled his eyes hard, and that did nothing but make me laugh even harder.

"Boy, if you don't shut up and leave this girl alone. If she don't want to do it, she doesn't have to."

"Speak for yourself. She's going to do this shoot for me whether she likes it or not. And if I'm paying her, I don't see why she would be turning it down. Now, I don't mean to sound harsh or nothing like that, but what you do?"

Tatum hit Marquis on the shoulder, and he looked at her with wide eyes.

"You don't have to answer that..."

"No, I know he didn't mean no harm. But currently nothing." I replied as I shrugged.

This issue too had been on my mind. The last thing I remembered was managing the club and stripping every now and again, but I knew that I didn't want to go back to doing that. Since I hadn't had any type of conversation with Kimani about where our relationship was going or whether there was still a relationship, I knew that I shouldn't be depending on his kindness for too much longer. I wasn't the type of chick that needed anybody for anything, but here I was waiting for a conversation to decide my future. Fuck that.

"You know what? If you're paying, I'm in. I need to figure out what to do with my life, and since ya'll think I got something, I guess modeling is as good a place as any to start."

"Yasss, bitch! I'm going to get with my marketing team this week and see what we can pull together. I've been wanting to revamp my whole marketing strategy, and you would be the perfect person to help me. Ooh! I'm too excited!"

Marquis started twerking in his seat, and Tatum and I started laughing. A few moments later the waitress came over and took our drink and food orders. Once she left, Marquis stood from his seat.

"Alright, I'll be back. I gotta use the little girl's room."

"I'm going too. I have a feeling we're going to be throwing back drinks for a while." Tatum stood, shaking her head.

I giggled and watched them walk away. I looked down at my phone to see if I had any missed calls or text from Kimani and was disappointed when I saw that I didn't. I was beyond frustrated at this point. He had shown so much emotion when we reconnected, but he hadn't put forth one ounce of effort to make sure I was cool after everything I went through. I wasn't even sure at this point if I should try harder to get him to focus on me or give him his space.

"Please don't freak out."

I jumped at the sound of his voice and braced myself by holding on to the arms of the chair. Fear engulfed me, and I wasn't sure why. I knew him, and I knew him intimately so why was I so scared? I felt his hand grasp mine, and my heart rate slowed. Still unsure, I turned towards him. He was still as handsome as ever with his light brown skin, sharp, brown eyes and strong jawline. His beard had grown a lot in the week or so that I had been gone and even though I could feel the worry and weariness emanating from his body, he still looked put together. Dressed in a pair of wheat colored cargo pants, a white t-shirt that skimmed over his muscular body perfectly and a pair of army green Huaraches. On his head, he wore a baseball hat in the same color as his sneakers and his only jewelry was his diamond studs. I was wary of him, but I couldn't deny the fact that he was still the very ruggedly handsome man that I had fallen for.

"Israel, I said finally releasing the breath that I had been holding in.

He tightened his grip on my hand when he started to notice that it was shaking.

"Why are you scared of me?"

My eyes bucked at his question. What the fuck did he mean? He had kidnapped me from a fucking hospital, erased my memory and trained me to kill the people that I had been closest to. If that wasn't enough to cause someone to be scared of him, then they had to be missing the fear gene.

"Why are you here? What do you want?" I asked nervously.

I looked around the restaurant hoping that Tatum and Marquis would come back soon. It was broad daylight outside, and I was terrified that he was going to slip something in my drink and throw me over his shoulder.

"I didn't come to scare you. I came because I miss you."

His eyes showed that he was telling the truth, but I still didn't trust him. He was a stranger to me. Everything that I thought I knew about him was concocted and covered in white lies that had snowballed into a big, boldface lie and I couldn't bring myself to believe him. But seeing him weakened and defeated me. The beating of my heart had finally slowed to its normal pace as I regained my confidence.

"You need to leave," I stated firmly. "You're a liar and a manipulator, and you cost me almost an entire year of my life. I don't trust you and whatever love I thought that I had for you was built on a mountain of bullshit that you forced me to believe. I don't miss you, desire you, love you, want you, need you or believe you. Your best bet is to get the fuck out my face before I scream to high heavens that my kidnapper is back."

The look in Israel's eyes after I told him off surprised me. It was like I could literally see his heart break into a million pieces right in front of me. I started to apologize, but Israel removed his hand from mine and took a deep breath. Pulling a card out of his pocket, he eased it onto the table before standing.

"I'm sorry, but I'm not giving up. I plan to spend the rest of my life making you understand how in love I am with you. I know I fucked up, but you know deep down that my feelings for you are something that I never have lied to you about. I know you think that nigga that you with is your soul mate or whatever but that nigga ain't even trying. So when you're tired of chasing behind a nigga that's too wrapped up in himself to care about you, give me a call. I'll always be here."

With that, he turned and walked away just as Tatum and Marquis returned to the table eyeing him down. I watched him leave while fingering the card he'd left.

Marquis snapped his fingers in front of my face. "Earth to Blu!"

"Huh? What'd you say?"

"Girl, I feel you. A man that damn delicious would have made me lose my breath too, Marquis stated before he broke out in Destiny's Child's "Lose my Breath."

Tatum howled, and I giggled a little, but my mind was elsewhere. Israel was right. I knew by looking in his eyes that the one thing he hadn't lied about were his feelings for me. But what was I supposed to do with that? Was I supposed to drop Kimani, who felt something like my soul mate to fall back into the arms of my fucking abductor? This was too crazy for me to handle. I wasn't making a decision one way or another at the moment; I was just going to get wasted with my new friends and hope that like a hangover, I would be able to cure it all in the morning.

Karma
September 2015

I had a plan. It was shaky at best, but hopefully, everything worked out because I was running out of time. Thank goodness part of my plan had allowed me to hustle up some money because I had begun to run out of that as well. But things had started to come together that day in the hospital.

I turned to leave Blaze's room, a plan slowly beginning to form in my brain. I was so caught up in my thoughts, that I ran smack dab into someone.

"The fuck?"

I hadn't just run into someone but I had also managed to slam my body right into the barrel of a gun. I grabbed my wounded stomach and walked backwards and into the room as the man holding the gun closed the door behind me. He was tall and stocky; built like you would imagine a bodyguard would be. He was the color of beach sand with a shiny bald head and a massive amount of facial hair. One of his eyes was damn near closed like that rapper Fetty Wap, while the other gleamed with a hint of evil and was black as tar. He could have been a very handsome man, but there was something off-putting about him that immediately made him dark and ugly;

a stark contrast from his light skin color and naturally handsome face.

"Who are you?"

My eyebrow raised at his high pitched voice. He sounded like a fucking cartoon character. I would have laughed out loud had the nigga not been holding a gun.

"Umm, I should be asking you that. Why are you up in a hospital waving a fucking gun around like the shit is normal?" I scoffed.

"You must be fucking crazy to question the person holding the gun like its normal," he retorted.

"So they say. So what's up? You gon' shoot me or nah because I've got shit to do today."

I was already fed up with this muthafucka and could care less that he had a gun. It would take me all of three seconds to have that gun out of his hand and at his forehead if he wanted to try me.

"You a friend of hers?" he questioned?

"Not hardly. She owes me something. But I can't get if from the bitch if she's dead. So I came to see how she was doing. The quicker she recovers, the quicker I get what I want."

I was done fooling around. Blaze was the obvious way to get at Grey. She had stolen his heart; that much was apparent by the rock he had put on her finger. So once this dizzy hoe snapped out of it, she was going to help me get what I wanted. Revenge.

"Hmm. Seems like Cadence owes a lot of people things," he said eyeing Blaze.

"Who?"

"Cadence. That's the name her mother gave her. She changed it to that other weird shit after she ran off with one million dollars of my money and left her newborn daughter in my care."

My eyes widened in shock. Who the fuck knew little Miss Put Together had all this damn baggage? This shit was juicy. I looked back at the man in front of me who had now lowered his gun. Quickly I deduced that I needed to try and remain on his good side. We both needed Blaze and needed her alive in order to get what we wanted, but I didn't need him trying to do his own separate thing and fucking up my plans. I needed Blaze to get to Grey, and I needed this big jolly green giant ass nigga to cooperate.

"Damn that's fucked up. But uh, let me holla at you real quick."

He looked at me curiously; well, at least I think he did. It was hard to tell with that fucked up ass eye he had.

"So check this out. You need Blaze and so do I. She's the only person that can get to someone for me, but she can't do it from here. I have a friend that could probably get her out of the hospital and to a safe location that you and I would have access to until we get what we want. But I need something first. Well, two things."

"Nothing comes without a price." He laughed. "What do you need, beautiful?"

I just knew this Cyclops looking ass nigga wasn't trying to hit on me. I was going to let it slide but he better chill.

"Well, first I need some cash. This shit ain't gon be easy or cheap so don't try and play me like you ain't balling. You let that bitch skate with a mil of your money and let her breathe for years, so you obviously ain't tripping on money."

I looked at him, and he nodded to continue.

"Secondly, I need a distraction. I need you to keep any and everyone from getting to her before I can get her out of here. Can you do that?"

"Easy money. You got that. But how do I know that I can trust you?"

"You can't trust nobody, including me. You gotta make your decisions based on how much you really want whatever it is that you need back from her. If you are willing to bet the house so that you can get it, do what I ask. Fuck trust. If not, *you can dip but just know I'm going to make it my personal mission to get Blaze before you do. It's your choice."*

A small smile broke across his face before he nodded his head again.

"Yo, you thorough as fuck, ma."

"My father taught me well. Now chill with the fucking pet names and shit. I don't want nothing you offering outside of what I just requested, One-Eyed Willie. But you can call me Karma."

After the conversation, we shook on it.

"Baron."

"Aight na', Baron. I need this shit done fast. Give me your number and I'll call you in two days once I'm ready for her to get the fuck up out of here.

We exchanged numbers and a day later he called to let me know that he already had something in motion to distract Grey from visiting Blaze. I had been to the hospital every day since to make sure that Blaze's condition hadn't changed and being a doting friend like the nurses now believed that I was. I had used a lifeline and phoned a friend; the only one I had left since I had burned hella bridges since being on the warpath to get revenge on Grey. The homie Trinity came through for me though and today was the day that we made our move.

I stood outside the hospital as I waited for the nurses to change shifts. Since my outburst, I had tried to get chummy with the nurses on staff, and thanks to my bomb ass acting skills, I had made friends with this bubbly white chick named Amber. As I waited for her to clock in, I called Trinity up.

"Hey girl, are you ready on your end?"

She responded with sarcasm. "Hey, Karma. How are you? I'm doing fine thanks for asking."

"Trinity, I don't have the time for your fucking dramatics."

"Well had you given me what I asked for then you wouldn't be on the receiving end of my sarcasm," she sighed. "Do you even know where he is?"

Damn, this bitch was getting on my nerves. She was so head over heels for Roman's ass that she couldn't concentrate to save her life. I had promised her that if she helped me get Blaze out of the hospital and into private care, then I would get Roman to reach out to her. She apparently had something important to talk to him about, but I could care less. Trinity was the only person that I could count on to make this call for me, and I would have promised her a three ring circus if that's what she wanted. Hell, I didn't have the slightest clue where Roman's ass was at but a fake

number or address was going to have to do as payment. I
needed Blaze out of this hospital.

"Of course, I know where he is. Stop sweating me, damn.
I'll get you in contact with him once you call the hospital.
Now are you ready on your end?"

"Yes," Trinity huffed.

"Good. I'll text you when I'm ready."

I hung up on her ass with a roll of my eyes and picked
up the two coffees that sat on top of my rental car. I took a
deep breath to get myself into acting mode and then
strutted into the hospital in search of my little dumb blonde.
I found her at the large desk right outside of Blaze's room
easing into her seat while running her mouth with the other
nurses. She looked up and saw me and a bright smile
covered her face.

"Hey, girlie! You back to see Blaze? I was just about to
call you."

I handed her the coffee in my hand, and she smiled in
appreciation.

"Call me for what? You know I don't get up here until
you get on shift. I can't stand none of these other hoes."

She laughed before taking a sip out of her cup. "I was
calling to tell you that Blaze is awake!"

Grey
September 2015

This shit was fucking with me man. How the fuck was me and these stupid ass niggas related? This shit ain't make no damn sense. This nigga's lived high off the fucking hog in a mansion in Miami and shit all his life while Kimani and I lived in the fucking projects. Our mother worked three fucking jobs just to take care of us and these weak ass pussies grew up with a silver spoon in their mouths. And don't even get me started on this muh'fucka, Jorge. You telling me that nigga, the one that brought me into the drug game, that laced me with product, that treated me like I was a part of his extended family was really my fucking father? Hell fucking no. I didn't believe that shit for a minute. Someone may have given ya nigga some bad information because this shit ain't add up at all. So fuck all that middle man shit I had Brandin and Cope on. I was going to go get answers from the people that I knew would be able to help me figure out the truth. The Royals.

Thing was, I had baby girl with me. I looked over at her and smiled to myself. Harmony was laid on the leather sofa with the chenille throw over her body; mouth open and drooling like a muthafucka. It was probably the best sleep she'd had in months. I didn't understand how I had become an Instant dad but nonetheless I had stepped up in Blaze's absence. I had a soft spot for kids even though I didn't have any and I didn't want Harmony left in the care of strangers. Even though she was a sweet girl, I could tell that she wasn't being treated well wherever she was at before she got to me. So now that she was in my care, I wasn't going to let nobody do her wrong.

I couldn't understand the situation even if I tried, and honestly, I hadn't attempted to. I had too much other shit on my mind to try and figure out if Harmony was really Blaze's daughter or her sister...shit or both and why she left her behind and failed to mention her to me. I didn't like secrets, so when Blaze woke her ass up, she was going to have to fucking explain. But for now, I was just going to roll with the punches and make sure baby girl was good.

The private jet that I had chartered to get us to Detroit was dope as fuck. If this had been a social call, a nigga would have been popping the champagne sitting in the mini fridge and enjoying myself; but right now I couldn't even think straight and adding alcohol to the mix would have made shit worse. I needed my mind clear to process the bullshit that went down.

"Another water, sir?"

The pretty, young flight attendant had been trying her best to show the fuck out. When I had boarded the plane with Harmony, she had been the picture of professionalism. But since take-off, she had unbuttoned her blouse almost down to her nipples, applied more makeup and let her long brown hair out of the bun that it was originally in. She was cute, no doubt, but she was way too thirsty for me. And while other niggas be out here fucking anything in a skirt, I was good. Blaze was my chick regardless of what bullshit she had done in her past. I had put a fucking ring on her finger for goodness sake. Wasn't no sticking my dick up in another chick. This dick was Blaze's for life. As long as she pulled through for a nigga, I didn't have a need to be dipping up in another chick.

"Nah, I'm good. How much longer we got?"

"We should be landing in about ten minutes, sir."

"Bet."

I stood up and went to take a piss. Once I had washed my hands, I returned to my seat and buckled up, preparing for landing. Twenty minutes later we arrived in the D. I stepped off the plane and took a deep breath. Wasn't shit like Detroit, man. As gritty and fucked up as it was, Detroit was home, and I lived and breathed it no matter where my body resided. Detroit would always have my heart.

I carried a still-sleeping Harmony in my arms and gently placed her inside of the waiting rental car. I wanted to stay low-key this trip, so I just got a Nissan Altima to cruise the city in. This was supposed to be an in and out trip so no need to be out here stunting. I needed to get back to my baby. I felt bad as fuck because I still hadn't seen her since she was taken to the hospital and that shit was weak and selfish. I had however asked Mizhani to stop by every day and give me updates. I had sent some flowers and balloons but to not actually be there holding her hand, telling her everything was going to be okay, was fucked up on my part. But I was going to stop the bullshit as soon as I got this information. After thanking the flight crew, I hopped in my whip and pulled off to see my people.

The Royals were a powerful family in Detroit. They had shit sewed up, east to west, north to fucking south, and the crazy thing about it was nobody knew they were running shit. Most people thought that they were a wealthy family who ran a lot of businesses in the city, but the truth was that they were a trill ass mafia family. I had worked under the Royals while I was living in the D but a few years back, they told me that they were getting a new connect and that I would need to cop from someone else. There was no love lost, and they continued to let me have control over my territories, but they put me in touch with Jorge and told me that I was on my own. It seemed a little off at the time, but I was a young nigga then. As long as my money was right and I could still slang my shit, I didn't care who I was copping from. Now, the move made sense if Jorge was really my fucking father. But the only way I would find out was by talking to them and seeing what was up.

After thirty minutes of driving, I pulled up to Butter's and tossed the keys to the valet. I pulled Harmony, who was just now waking up, out of the backseat and we walked into the restaurant. The shit was nice as fuck. I hadn't been to Butter's place because while I was living in the D, it was still under construction but now that I finally had the time to visit, I had to admit this shit was live. Beans and Cornbread ain't have shit on Butter's.

On the inside, Butter's looked like you were sitting in someone's house. It had that homey feel, but it was also luxe as fuck. To the left was the dining room. There were wood tables and chairs and a long family style booth along the far wall. There were a few high top tables here and there, and they were decorated with gold linens, white china, and expensive silverware. Straight ahead was the living room. There was a big, double-sided, electric fireplace that stood in the middle of the living room area and around it were plush couches that sat a little higher than normal and tables that met the height of the couches to create a more comfortable dining experience. To the right was the bar/lounge area. The bar was tall and laid in cherry wood with gold high top bar stools. There were a few more tables in this area and TV's along the wall behind the bar. If you walked through the bar area, you were greeted by the open kitchen. It looked just like a kitchen in an expensive home but functioned like a restaurant kitchen. I had never seen anything like it in my life. I was taking notes for damn sure.

"Grey!"

I turned towards the sweet voice and instantly smiled. Butter came rushing towards me, her hips and titties jiggling the whole way. It was hard for me to keep my eyes off her voluptuous shape; she was stacked like a fucking brick house. She was gorgeous too. My young ass had tried to get on Butter when I was poppin' in the D, but she wasn't even having it. I laughed to myself as she approached me and wrapped me up in a hug. When she pulled back and crouched down to Harmony's level, Harmony hid behind my leg.

"Is this your daughter, Grey? She's beautiful."

"Thank you."

I didn't feel like going into detail about Harmony because the truth was, I didn't know the details my damn self. So I just opted not to say shit else about the subject.

"It's good to see you, B." I nodded my head as I looked around. "Your restaurant is lit. Real innovative shit."

"Thank you," she blushed. "Mama is upstairs waiting on you. C'mon."

She turned around and led me to the back of the restaurant where she pushed on a panel that revealed a secret door. My eyebrow arched. Butter smiled knowingly.

"I'll take Miss...."

"Harmony."

"Miss *Harmony* to the kitchen with me. We can make some cupcakes. Is that cool, Harmony?"

Harmony instantly looked up at me for approval. I winked at her, causing her to smile.

"Chocolate ones?" she asked shyly.

Butter grinned. "The chocolatiest ones."

Harmony nodded her head happily and reached for Butter's extended hand. She patted me on the shoulder before walking away. I turned towards the door and took a deep breath. It was time to get some muh'fucking answers.

Kimani
September 2015

"Here. Change into this."

We were currently at The Association, a club in downtown LA about to film for the reality show. The stylist on set handed me a hanger of clothes and pointed in the direction of the men's room. Too consumed by my thoughts to care, I took the clothes and walked away. This shot was supposed to be me chilling and popping bottles with a few other castmates and some kind of drama was going to pop off. Yeah, this reality shit was as scripted as a regular ass show. All of the drama and meetings and run-ins were staged. None of that shit happened by coincidence. The producers needed action and drama, and there was no other guaranteed way to get it than to create it. So here we are.

I arrived on set wearing casual basketball shorts and tee, and ten minutes later, I came out of the men's room back on set rocking clothes supplied by one of the show's sponsors. They were decent but not better than anything in my closet. They had me in a pair of navy blue slacks, a fitted white t-shirt and a cream colored blazer. There was a silk printed pocket square that was the same color of my pants sitting in my breast pocket; on my feet were a pair of chocolate colored leather loafers. It wasn't the designer shit I was used to, but this shit was how the reality shows stayed popping. And they were cutting my check, so fuck it.

I walked over to the section that they had roped off for us and dapped up my co-stars, Ty'Ron Boyd and Kelsey "KelC" Chalmers. Ty'Ron was the number one draft pick in the NBA. He'd played for Duke University and had killed shit his whole college career and was just now getting his professional ball career off the ground. KelC was a music producer who had had produced damn near all of the current songs on the fucking radio station. He was like the new DJ Mustard. I rocked with them niggas the long way; they were cool as fuck. Now this nigga, Junip, that was currently sitting in the corner on his phone, he could kick rocks. He was this cocky ass up and coming actor that thought the sun rose and set on his black ass. Ol' ashy black, Tyrese looking ass muh'fucka. He thought that he was the new age Morris Chestnut and shit and acted like he was better than the rest of us because he had played in a million dollar movie. I hate to break it to the nigga but he only had about ten lines and nobody even remembered his wack ass.

A few moments later, the ladies walked up looking good as fuck. They were all dressed in tight ass dresses and sky high heels; breasts and booty everywhere. Ivory came over and sat next to me with a smile on her face. She was a dope ass white girl with hella swag. She could sing her ass off too. I would bet money that she was going to be the next thing popping on the R&B charts. Rayne and Silver made their way through the crew giving out hugs. They were sisters who were the dopest DJ's on the scene right now. They were so in demand that they were booked for a year solid. They were the new addition to the cast this season. Feline was the last to enter the booth on her rah rah shit per usual. Feline was a videographer. She was a contemporary visionary and had directed some of the illest videos and short films that I'd seen. She was a loud and wild female, but she was always on her shit. She gave me a hug and then went and sandwiched herself between Junip and Ivory.

O'Lessa, the producer, came sauntering over to us a few moments later. A collective sigh was released from the group because that bitch was a handful and half. I knew when I signed up for the show that drama was necessary, but O'lessa lived for it. She breathed ratchet behavior and would sometimes go to extreme lengths to get the melodramatic scene that she was looking for.

"Good evening, folks! We've got a long night ahead so brace yourselves!"

I rolled my eyes and checked my phone. I had two texts; one from Blu and the other from Grey, which was a shock. I hadn't heard from that angry ass nigga since I hit him with the secret I had been holding onto. All he said in the text was: In Detroit. His text just reminded me that while I was fooling around on set of this reality show, I hadn't made one move to get them sucka ass niggas that were gunning for us. I just hadn't had the time. On top of the reality show, Steph had me doing a test read for a scripted series, and I had two modeling gigs on the back burner. I was swamped. And don't even get me started on Clappers.

The second text from Blu was her asking me when I was going to be home. I shook my head at that one. I had really been slipping when it came to Blu. I finally had her back in my life but with my hectic ass schedule and finding Roman and Israel in the back of my mind, I had let our relationship fall by the wayside. I could tell that she was trying not to nag, but in the same token, she felt neglected, and that's definitely not how I wanted her to feel. I made a mental note to tell Steph to block my schedule this weekend so that I could spend time with her. I couldn't have Blu leave my life again and me be the cause of it. She was the soul that lived inside of me, and I couldn't be out in this cold world soulless.

"Alright, so when the music starts, everyone needs to turn up. Interact with each other, dance, drink, whatever. But try and stay off your phones. Our special guest will be making their entrance shortly, and I don't want to have to do too many takes of this."

O'Lessa's eyes lingered on me, and I smirked. That midget bitch wanted the D so bad, but there wasn't a damn thing that she could do to get me to fuck her messy ass. I sent Grey a simple "Ok" back and then hit Blu, apologizing for my absence once again, before sliding my phone into my back pocket.

"Places everyone! Let's make this juicy!" O'lessa shouted before turning around to get behind the cameras.

Ivory turned to me and rolled her eyes. I laughed at her obvious annoyance. She leaned down to whisper in my ear.

"I can't wait to be done shooting. I doubt I'll be back for a season three."

"You and me both. I got what I needed out of the deal."

She nodded her head in agreement as the music started to play. Drake and Future's "Where Ya At" blasted out of the nearby speakers and the extras that surrounded us, started to move their bodies to the music. I noticed the red light on the camera, so I took a deep breath and did the job that I was paid to do. I poured up a cup of Ciroc Apple and added a dash of apple juice, then lifted the drink to my lips as I bobbed my head to the music. I squinted my eyes and saw a shapely woman coming into view; she was making her way over to our table. I damn near spit my drink all over the poor girl below me as I realized who it was—fucking Vicious!

As if my night couldn't get any worse, the persistent thirst bucket who wouldn't be able to catch a clue if it was the common cold, waltzed her ass inside the club. Her Cheshire cat-like smile made me cringe. She was a thorn in my fucking side. Why wouldn't she just disappear? There was no denying the fact that she was batting a thousand in the looks department. Her signature wild, curly hair framed her face and the silver sequined jumpsuit that she wore looked as if it had been poured over her body like paint. Vicious was killing every single female in here, but she was death in designer, and I didn't want to be anywhere near her.

"Cut! Cut! Muthafuckin' cut!" I yelled, before slamming my glass down on the table.

My castmates cleared a path so that I could escape from the booth we sat in and get to O'lessa's trifling ass. Vicious placed herself in my path, but I quickly sidestepped her and made my way to O'Lessa.

"What the fuck is she doing here? My contract states that I will get to choose my love interest, if any, on this show and I definitely didn't choose her parched ass."

"True. You contract does state that. But as the producer of this show I have to make sure that we get ratings. Vicious, the top charting, R&B diva that she is, is going to get us those. So while she doesn't have to be your love interest, she is a new cast member. So walk your tight ass back over to the VIP booth and do your job."

As badly as I wanted to slap the shit out of this broad, that wasn't even in my character. So I smirked and nodded my head before letting her know that she would be hearing from Steph bright and early in the morning. I walked back over to my section, a pounding headache brewing. Vicious was hot on my heels.

"You're not happy to see me?" she asked as she tugged on my arm.

I ripped my arm out of her grasp and scowled. "Fuck no. I told your ass I didn't want to be bothered, but you got rocks for brain cells."

"I'm here to get a check. So don't...."

I cut her off with the quickness. "Man, get outta here with that bullshit. You came on this show because you still want this pipe." I grabbed my dick through my jeans for emphasis. "The pipe can't even get hard for your begging ass no more. Fuck outta my face, Vicious."

"You will *not* embarrass me on national TV, Kimani!" she screamed.

"You embarrassing ya'self, baby girl. I didn't ask you to come on this show. Matter of fact, I asked your delusional ass to stay away from me. I don't know why you thought a few reality show cameras were going to change that. You brought this on yourself, remember that."

With that, I turned my back to her, picked up the glass of liquor and threw it down my throat. I blocked out Vicious for the rest of the night and turned up with the rest of the reality show fam, minus Junip, who sat his moody ass in the corner the entire night. By the time the cameras stopped rolling, a nigga was faded. My eyes were low, and my body was slumped. I could walk and shit, but there was no way that I was driving anywhere.

Staggering over to the door of the club, I pushed it open only to be greeted by a swarm of paparazzi. Flashing lights erupted, and my hand immediately flew towards my face. I could tell that they were hurling questions at me, but I couldn't comprehend anything that they were saying. I was definitely lit. I attempted to push through the people, but my body was weakened by the liquor. Suddenly, I felt a hand on my lower back, and the swarm of people immediately parted like the red sea.

"Excuse us! Move, please! No questions tonight!"

I might have been inebriated, but I knew her voice even in my darkest haze. Vicious had come from inside the club and was now ushering me through the crowd. I wanted to push her ass off me, but I was too drunk to fight her off. A nigga just wanted to lay down. As soon as we reach the curb, her black SUV pulled up. The driver hopped out and opened the door, and waited for us to get in. Once I was inside, Vicious slid in next to me and closed the door. I could feel her hands roam my body as the driver hopped back into the car.

"Where to, ma'am?"

"My place, please."

Fuck! This wasn't going to be good at all.

Blu
September 2015

The incessant ringing of my cell phone caused me to jerk upright in the bed and answer with an attitude.

"What?"

"Baby, why you yelling? Shit my head hurts," Kimani groaned into the phone.

"Oh, I don't know. Maybe because it's eight in the damn morning and you aren't home from last night!"

I hated that I sounded like a nagging ass girlfriend, but Kimani had me fucked up. I was already sick of him being gone all the damn time, but at least he was coming home. Last night was the first night I had slept alone in God knows how long and I was pissed about it.

"Blu, baby...I'm sorry. I got drunk last night and I..."

"Whatever Kimani. We'll talk about it when you get home. In the meantime, I want to get some sleep." I wouldn't dare try and hide the irritation I was feeling. He deserved every last shred of it. "I was up half the damn night waiting for someone that never showed."

"Well, that's the thing. I need you to do me a favor."

I bolted out of the bed and stood to my feet, anger flooding my body. "So let me get this straight. You ignore me for weeks and stay out all night getting drunk with God knows who and you call me at 8 in the morning on a Saturday to ask me to do you a favor? You done lost your rabbit ass mind!" I yelled.

"Blu! Shit! I don't have time for all this back and forth. I apologized, and I'll be home, and like you said, we can talk about it then. But for now, I need you to calm your ass down and follow my instructions, damn!"

I wanted to cuss him out for having the nerve to be mad, but instead, I bit the inside of my cheek and waited for him to tell me what he needed me to do.

"The hospital called me and told me that Blaze, Grey's girl, is awake. I can't get in touch with that nigga, so can you please go up there and check on her and talk to the doctors? I told them that you're a friend of the family."

I remained quiet because I was unsure if what I was thinking was going to rush out my mouth prematurely and cause further tension. I didn't know Blaze from Adam and after the stunt that Kimani pulled, I didn't owe him shit, so I really didn't feel the need to sacrifice my Saturday to do him any favors. But the girl *was* shot and nearly died, and if her man wasn't there to see her and console her, I guess she needed somebody to represent in the meantime. Damn me and my kind heart.

"Hello? Blu?" Kimani paused when he didn't receive a response. "Did she hang up...?"

"I'm here, I finally said. "Fine. I will go check on her but—"

"Thank you!" he exclaimed, cutting me off. "I'll text you the information."

"Kimani, I'm not done with you."

"I brought bagels!" a melodic female voice sung on his end of the phone.

"Who the fuck—"

"I gotta go, B. It's not what you think, I promise. I love you."

I didn't realize that he had hung up on my ass until I heard the three little beeps. *Ohh*, so that's how he wants to play it, huh? His ass was in for a rude awakening. I was not about to sit and play boo boo the goddamn fool while he went and did whatever the hell he wanted to do. Granted, because of his schedule we hadn't really gotten to discuss our expectations of each other, but I didn't think I'd have to explain that I wouldn't tolerate blatant disrespect. But I could show him better than I could tell him.

Throwing my phone back on the charger, I stripped out of my PJ's and hopped in the shower, anger still brewing. An hour later, I was dressed and got ready to run to the hospital. I had thrown on a pair of plain black leggings, a black Dimepiece cropped hoodie and a pair of Riccarcdo Tisci Air Force 1 high top sneakers. I had used my curling wand to throw some waves in my shoulder length, jet black hair and did a light beat on my face. I looked casual and cute, but irritation was still present and dampening my mood. The only thing that could get me out of my funk was some music, so I grabbed the keys to the Range Rover that had been sitting unused in Kimani's garage and left the house.

The thirty-five-minute ride to the hospital with Eric Bellinger blasting did just the opposite of what I needed it to do. Instead of lifting my mood, it caused me to sink further into my feelings. I wished that a man loved me the way that Eric Bellinger seemed to love whomever he was singing about in those songs. As much as I had been scared of being loved deeply by someone before, having gone through the shit that I had gone through recently, I wanted nothing more than unconditional love. I longed for someone to care about my happiness as much as their own.

Tears started to pool in my eyes as I sat in the hospital parking lot, staring aimlessly out of the window. The realization of my situation settled in causing the tears to fall without effort. I was living with a man that I couldn't remember being with and who was currently too busy to make an effort to get me to remember him. And if he decided that he didn't want to put forth an effort, or that he didn't care enough about me and whatever we had before to make it work, then I was screwed. I had no one. No family, no friends, no man. No one that I could call on to talk to, to depend on, or to rescue me if I was in trouble. Kimani had made it extremely obvious that I was nothing more than an afterthought, and he was all that I had. So I was out here naked, and it had never been more obvious.

Quickly, I wiped away the tears and pulled some napkins from the glove compartment to prevent my mascara from running. All this soft shit was going to have to stop. I knew that before all this shit went down, I was as independent as they came. I had taken care of myself without the help of anyone else and that hadn't changed. If I could do it then, I could do it now. The reason I was crying over some damn song like a little bitch was because my heart felt as though it changed. Emotions were bursting out of me, and I couldn't control them. This wasn't like me. Something had to have happened to make me feel like I needed or even deserved someone, and I'm guessing Kimani was the reason. I loved him and his inability to make me feel like he felt the same way was hurting me. But fuck it. Blu was capable of loving herself way better than anyone else could.

I took a deep breath and exited the car. I activated the alarm and walked into the hospital, stopping at the front desk to get directions to Blaze's room. Before I made it to the elevator, I stopped inside the gift shop and grabbed the girl some flowers. I perused the selection of bouquets, thinking about how awkward this was probably going to be. Suddenly, I heard my name being called. I turned in the direction of the voice and had to do a double take because I was sure that my mind was playing games with me. She didn't look the same, but she didn't look that different either. One thing was for sure; she was looking damn good to be a fucking dead bitch.

Gone was her long, wavy black hair; it had been replaced by a sharp, blonde ombre bob that had been flat ironed straight. I could tell that she had lost some weight because her hips and thighs were significantly slimmer as was her face. The most noticeable things about her were the burns on her face. Whomever her plastic surgeon was had done a good job at fixing most of them but anyone who knew her before could see the difference in her face. And even though she was in a hospital, she was dressed like she was about to walk a runway in Paris. She donned a khaki green, military-inspired fitted dress, a bomb pair of Stuart Weitzman strappy sandals in a cognac color and gold jewelry. She cat walked over to me, her ivory snakeskin Birkin bag swinging in the cradle of her arm, while I tried to shake off my surprise.

"Well, if it isn't my bestie, Blu Buckley."

She reached out for a hug, which automatically put me on guard because the Nakami I knew was not a touchy feely person. I gently patted her back and quickly released myself from her embrace.

"Nakami...you're...how are you....what the fuck?"

I noticed that she cringed slightly when I said her name and thought that was odd. She produced a strained smile before speaking.

"It's been a while. Where you been, boo?"

I looked at her quizzically. Had this broad truly lost her marbles? From what Kimani told me, Nakami had tried to kill me because she had thought that I had slept with Grey and gotten pregnant. Never mind all that, this hoe was supposed to be dead. Well, at least that's what Kimani told me. So either he was lying, or Nakami had truly risen from the dead.

"Fuck all that, Kami. Aren't you supposed to be dead? Everyone thinks you died in that house fire."

Surprise danced in her eyes until they abruptly iced over. "The funny thing about fires is that they tend to burn all the evidence including bodies. Leaves a lot of room for speculation. But kudos to you. I see that you're getting your memory back. Thought that was going to be irreversible," she said, with a smirk. She had dropped the façade, and I was ready for this bitch.

Ignoring her snide remarks, I stepped closer to her. "Why are you here? Does Grey and Kimani know that you're alive?"

She smiled widely and slowly took a few steps towards me, closing the small distance that had stood between us. Running her tongue across her teeth, she paused before chuckling a little.

"Oh, Blu. You're so fucking lost in the sauce. Always have been, always will be. This is a long game that I'm playing. So no, that nigga and his bitch ass brother don't know I'm alive, and you're going to keep it that way."

"Why the fuck would I do that. I'm telling everyone who will listen. Shit, I probably need to tell one of these nurses in here so they can run you over to the looney bin where you belong."

I started to walk past her, but she quickly grabbed my wrist, viciously digging her stiletto nails into my flesh. I could feel my skin break from the deathly pressure she was applying.

"Who's going to believe you, bitch? You don't have proof the first that I'm alive. Plus your memory has been fucked with so anybody that even stops to listen to you is going to think that it's your fragmented ass memory piecing shit together out of order."

She released her grip on my wrist for a second and then she plunged her nails back into my skin, making me take a harsh breath.

"You're going to go visit Blaze like you were asked to do, and you'll go home like everything is all good, or I'll call in reinforcements on that ass."

Even though I was in pain, I managed to force out a laugh. She was really tripping if she thought that she was scaring me into keeping my mouth shut. This bitch was out in a public place with no help or backup, lying through her damn teeth.

"I'm not scared of your ass, bitch, I hissed.

She dug her nails further into my skin, causing me to bite down on my lip. The pain was killing me, but I was trying not to show it.

"You should be. If it wasn't for Roman saving your dumb ass, you would've been dead behind the bullets I put in your body." She shook her head. I can't believe how bad my aim was. Best believe that if you utter one word about me to Kimani, I will sic Roman and Israel on you so quick that you won't have a chance to see it coming. Keep your mouth closed and I'll consider leaving you and Kimani be. The only one I really want is Grey. I guess I could spare your life to claim his."

This bitch was out of her mind. I knew that Nakami wasn't working with a full deck when we were friends, but I never suspected that she was this fucking twisted. Something about Grey had brought out this demented side of her, and if she thought that I was going to allow her to claim another life while I was still breathing and had the ability to warn a brother, she didn't remember who I was. I was loyal if nothing else, and although Kimani seemed to be playing games, he'd been more loyal to me than anyone I could remember. But I was going to let this bitch think that I was scared so that I could get the fuck out of here.

"I don't want to fucking die, so I'll keep your little secret. But whatever you plan on doing, you better do the shit fast."

She yanked me closer to her body. "Don't fucking threaten me, bitch. I do what the fuck I want and on my own time."

Dropping my purse to the floor, I used my free hand to grab ahold of her arm tightly. I didn't have quite the grip that she had on me, but it should have been enough to let her know that I was not about to play with her ass.

"Nakami, fuck you and fuck your time. Do what you gotta do and do the shit fast."

I jerked my arm out of her tight grip, scratching my shit in the process, and bent down to pick up my purse. As I proceeded to walk out of the gift shop empty-handed, I heard Nakami call after me.

"What?!"

"I just wanted to let you know Nakami really *is* dead. You can call me Karma. And you know what they say about karma."

I didn't even bother with a response. I just walked out shaking my head. What the fuck had happened to her?

Grey
September 2015

I lifted the bottle to my lips, tilted my head back and let the liquid slide down my throat. It burned deliciously and like a fiend, I repeated the process, willing the burning sensation to cover the pain that I was in right now. I had met with Gertrude and Kane less than 24 hrs ago, and the news I received still had me in shock. They were my brothers. My fucking brothers! As I went to throw back another shot, I replayed the conversation I had with my old boss.

"Kendrick! It's so good to see you, baby." Gertrude extended her arms for a hug.

I swaggered across the room and wrapped her up in my arms, happy to see the OG gangsta. Gerdy was like the grandmother I never knew except she was on some mafia shit. I loved her like she was my flesh and blood and I hoped that she could tell me that this bullshit Brandin and Cope had found out about Roman and Israel was a damn lie. It would hurt my muthafuckin' soul if I found out that Gerdy had kept some shit like this from me.

I walked over to Butter's desk where Kane was seated and dapped him up before I took a seat on the fancy couch by the wall. Silence engulfed the room as we all sat staring at each. I let out a small laugh, amused by how awkward it already was. This only meant that whatever a nigga was about to hear, he wasn't going to like in the least bit.

I looked at Gerdy and then Kane, neither of their expressions were readable. "So what's good, Gerdy? Ya'll find some information for me?"

"Yeah, Kendrick. We got something for you."

I smiled a little at Gertrude calling me by my government. She was never one for nicknames. She was only calling your ass by your God-given name, no exceptions. She was the only one that ever called Butter by her real name. She was old school like that.

"Aight, lay it on me."

Gertrude walked over to the desk and took a seat on its corner. I stared at her, waiting for her to drop the bomb. Instead, she nodded her head at Kane. He grabbed a folder from the desk and handed it to me. I flipped it open, and the first thing I saw was a picture of a beautiful light skinned lady. She was fucking gorgeous. She kinda looked like my momma, but her nose was more slender, and her eyes were more green than brown. She had long, wild curly hair and a wide smile full of perfect white teeth.

"Who's this?" I held up the picture so that Gerdy and Kane could see.

"That's your mother."

I looked at the picture again and laughed.

"No, I mean, they kinda look similar but that ain't her. Her nose was a little wider, and she ain't have no green ass eyes."

Gerdy got up from her seat on the edge of the desk and sat next to me. Her hand landed on my shoulder and for some reason, my heart rate sped up. I was getting the feeling that I was about to hear the ultimate bullshit, and I wasn't prepared for it.

"That's your mother, hunny. Her name was Dinah, and she was the love of Jorge's life."

"Naw, man. My momma name is Nylah. This ain't her, OG."

"The woman you knew as your mother was your aunt. Your mother's sister."

I looked at Gerdy, confused, before I looked back down at the picture in my hand.

"My aunt? My fucking aunt?" I asked, stunned.

My eyes remained on the picture in my hand as I tried to comprehend what she was telling me. Anger started to bubble inside as I began to feel like my whole life was a lie. Either that or niggas was lying to me now.

"Now, I know this is going to be hard for you. You're going to want to cuss my old ass out, and while I don't blame you for having that instinct, I'm asking you politely to hold your tongue. I consider you family, but I will not hesitate to fuck your yellow ass up if you come at me reckless. You hear me?"

Gertrude grabbed at my chin and turned my head so that we were staring in each other's eyes. I ground my teeth in an effort to calm myself down, but the shit wasn't working. I didn't want to snap on Gerdy but there wasn't nothing about this story I was going to like. I could feel it.

"Damnit, Kendrick. I'm talking to you! Can you be calm while I tell you what happened, or do I need to get some goons in here to make sure you don't pop stupid? I love you, and I would hate to do it, but I will kill you if you let your temper get the best of you. Now, answer me, boy. Can you be calm about this?"

I respected her G, but I could tell that this conversation wasn't going to end well. I wanted to promise that I wouldn't fuck some shit up behind whatever it was she was about lay on a nigga, but I ain't into making promises that I can't keep. I would refrain from going ape on Gerdy but that was only out of respect. I couldn't say the same for the inanimate objects around the room. Butter would just have to be mad if my temper reached that peak.

"Yeah, man. I'm cool."

Gertrude finally let my chin go and nodded her head.

"Alright now. That woman in the picture is your mother, Dinah Summers and like I was saying before, she was the love your father's life. Jorge was next in line to inherit his father's business, but he went and fell in love with a black woman. She was damn near clear like you and your brother, but the fact that she had any African American in her blood was enough for your grandfather, Alberto, to be pissed the hell off. Not to mention that whore that your father was engaged to."

"Wait a minute. How do you even know that nigga? What role did you play in any of this?" I interrupted her.

"I'm getting to that son. Just hold tight," She fussed. "Liliana, the woman that your father was engaged to, found out about you and your mother and went and snitched to Jorge's father out of anger. His father had already warned him of the consequences of continuing to see Dinah, but he was a man in love. There was no threat dangerous enough to make him stop seeing her. But after Liliana told his father, things went to hell. He snatched the empire that Jorge had been preparing to head his entire life and then Liliana turned up pregnant. Fearing for the stability of his new family, Jorge approached his father to get back into his good graces."

"And that bitch ass nigga sacrificed my mother for money. Ol' weak as bitch!" I shot up out of my seat, rage surging through my body like it was being fed through an IV.

Gertrude grabbed at my arm, and her strong ass pulled me back down to the couch.

"Sit yo ass down, Kendrick. I ain't done."

My breaths quickened as I tried to contain my anger. How could a man trade the woman that was supposed to be the love of his life for anything let alone some mu'fucking money? If he was a real hustler, he would have provided for his family by any means necessary and said fuck his racist ass daddy!

"Anyway, he went to talk to his father about getting the empire back. Jorge only had a sister and she wasn't fit to run the empire, so he knew that if he made a deal to leave Dinah alone, his father would hand him back the family business with no problem. But he had plans to snuff his father out once he had the business back, but it was a plan that would take him some time. So he moved Dinah to Michigan and placed her under my protection. Otis Sr. copped from Alberto long before B came in the picture and we were implicitly trusted by Alberto and his family. We were good enough to make money for his ass, but apparently not good enough to bear his family name. The fucking nerve. Anyway, for the first two years of your life, you wanted for nothing. Jorge set your mother up

beautifully, and she took the best care of you. He frequently took trips to visit and on one of those trips, your brother was conceived. He had since married Liliana to keep up appearances with for your grandfather, but he was extremely close to getting from under Alberto's thumb and out of the loveless marriage with Liliana."

As Gertrude paused, I leaned forward. I had been hanging on her every word. This shit was playing out like an urban fiction novel, and I was anxious to know the rest of the damn story.

"Soon after he found out about Dinah being pregnant again, he learned that Liliana was pregnant too. With twin boys. He was heartbroken and happy at the same time. Happy that he had more children to bear his name and sad that it meant that he would have to deal with Liliana for another 18 years. He could have gotten rid of her, but he himself had grown up without a mother and never wanted his children to have to suffer the same type of childhood he had. So he continued his plan to kill his father, but after your mother had Kimani, he had to break the news to your mother that he still couldn't be with her because of the twins."

Gertrude shook her head as tears started to well up in her eyes. Fuck! I knew that whatever came out her mouth next was going to fucking kill me.

"I ain't never seen a woman so heartbroken in my life. You could feel the sadness and the pain radiating off her body. Oh, honey, I couldn't even take it. She came to me and asked me to protect her babies. I didn't know what she was talking about, but we had grown pretty close since she'd moved to Michigan and I loved you and your brother as if you were my own, so I agreed. But Lord knows that I didn't know what I had agreed to."

Gertrude took a deep breath as Kane came out of nowhere with a glass of water. She accepted it, took a swig, and handed it back to Kane who sat back down behind the desk.

"Nylah, your aunt, found your mother two days later. She had swallowed a whole damn bottle of sleeping bills. Now I liked your mother a lot, and I don't mean to speak ill of the dead, but that was some weak shit she did. I loved Otis to the moon and back, but if he had left me, I would have lived on if for nothing else, my baby's sake. But your mother was consumed with love for your father and that love ruined her. So your aunt took custody of ya'll after she committed suicide and told me and Jorge to stay the hell away. She didn't want anything to do with us or our money she just wanted to raise ya'll and forget everything else. She didn't care if she had to struggle or work twelve jobs, she wanted to stay away from

any and everything that had caused her sister harm. I tried my best to look out for you and your brother, but Nylah flat out refused."

Tears had managed to escape from my eyes and roll down my face. This was bullshit, man! I grew up thinking that my aunt was my mother and the woman that had birthed me was so fucked up behind a man that she hadn't had the strength to ride that shit out for the sake of her kids. Ultimately, my real mother loved a nigga more than she loved her children and finding that out hurt more than anything. It was bullshit, and I knew that if I hadn't promised Gerdy that I would keep my emotions at bay, I would've already set fire to some shit. I was beyond angry. Gertrude could sense it; my heavy breathing and my shaking leg gave me away. She placed a hand on my leg hoping to calm the shaking.

"Kendrick, listen to me. Your aunt did the best that she could. But she had so much anger and bitterness in her heart because of your mother's death that I believe that she just didn't have the capacity to love ya'll the way that ya'll needed her to. I want you to know that despite the odds, I was so damn proud when you and your brother graduated from college. And even though you had all the book smarts anyone could ask for, I knew that you were more like us...like me and your father...than your mother. You were a hustler from birth, *and it was only a matter of time before you followed in your father's footsteps."*

"Man, fuck him!" I shouted.

"Watch your mouth, boy! As much as you may not believe it, your father loved your ass! Your brother too!"

I stood up abruptly causing Gertrude to flinch.

"How you can you sit there and let that shit come out your mouth? That nigga had 22 years to get at me! 22 fucking years, yo!" I exclaimed, beating my hand against my chest with every word. "That bitch made nigga ain't love me!"

Gertrude got up and grabbed a hold of my arms roughly, shaking me in the process. "You listen to me, and you listen good. Your father loved you, Kendrick. Immensely."

"Man..."

I tried to dismiss her, but she held firm. "He kept up with your every move. Every perfect test score, every basketball game, every—"

I cut her off. "That don't mean shit! When we went days without eating, where was he then? When I had to wear dirty ass, Levi's from the thrift store and then pass them shits down to my brother two years later, where was he then? When a nigga needed his fucking father to be a man, where was he, Gerdy? That shit don't count, B!"

My voice had started to grow hoarse from all the yelling I was doing. She could keep that weak ass explanation. The truth was that nigga was too busy with his other family to think about us.

"He wanted to see you. But before he could get to your grandfather, he died of massive kidney failure. In his will he had left his fortune to Jorge but only if he followed the stipulations that were written into his will. He was to marry Lilian and stay married to her until all of their children turned 18. And he was to have no contact with any of you. If it was found that he had gone against either of the stipulations, everything that had been left to him would become his sister's. He couldn't, baby. He just couldn't."

My body dropped back down onto the couch, and I buried my head in my hands. Emotions swirled inside me like a tornado as I tried to deal with everything that Gerdy had laid on me.

After a nigga had calmed down, she gave me the rundown on the family that I never knew I had. Kane had pulled up Kimani and I's real birth certificate that listed Jorge as our father and Dinah as our mother. He told me about Roman and Israel and their sister who was currently in a vegetative state after the FEDS had bombed the house looking for Jorge behind what my brother did. They ran down all the information that they had, and I sat there and absorbed it until I couldn't take no more. I mumbled "thank you" before walking out the door and skirting off with my mind heavy. Why, Lord?

A nigga was out here hurting. It was too much going on, and I didn't know how I was going to be able to shuffle through it. These niggas after me were my fucking brothers. *Blood fucking brothers*. And their father was also mine. It fucked me up to know that I had been in the presence of my father plenty of times, shook hands with the nigga, broke bread with the nigga, and I was none the wiser. Shit, a nigga didn't even know he was Spanish and shit. I just thought....man, fuck what I thought. None of that shit was valid now.

I took another shot straight from the bottle and wiped the corners of my mouth with my fingers. I knew that I couldn't continue to function like this. In the hours since I left Gerdy, I had polished off a full bottle of Hennessey, and a nigga was straight numb. I just wanted to forget that I had even found all that stuff out, and to go back to the way things were before I learned that nothing that I knew my life to be was the truth. But I couldn't. I had Harmony to think about, and I had to get back to Blaze. Not only that, I needed to get up with my dumbass brother and find my other fucking brothers before any more blood was shed. This shit needed to end.

I lifted my hand to toss back the final swig that was swirling around inside of the bottle, and I heard my phone vibrate against the loose change I'd left in my pants pocket. Rolling my eyes, I set the bottle down by my feet and fished my phone out. I could have sworn that I had placed that bitch on mute an hour ago just to get some peace but apparently I'd chosen vibrate instead. My phone had been ringing incessantly and I was two seconds from throwing that bitch into the wall. If it wasn't Brandin or Cope, it was Kimani calling me back to back. Also, the detectives on Blaze's case had been blowing me up, trying to get me to come in for an interview, but I had asked the Royals to use their connections with the police to get them off my back for a hot minute while I figured things out. When I say the Royals are well connected, I'm not exaggerating in the least.

My phone vibrated again. *What the fuck?* There wasn't one person that I wanted to talk to at the moment, not even Blaze. Glancing down at the screen, I saw who it was and groaned. I had been spinning the shit out of the OG, but she continued to call. *It must be important.* I sucked up my irritation and slid my finger across the screen to accept the call.

"Nine, what's good?"

Roman
September 2015

I paced the floor angrily, stopping periodically to look down at my phone. Nothing. This bitch was going to make me hurt her. I'd held up my end of the bargain and gotten Vicious out of her fucking contract, but this non-singing ass hoe was dragging her feet with Kimani. I should've waited until she had secured the meet with that nigga to make good on what I had promised her but that would have left me too much work to do. Instead, I extended a professional courtesy, thinking that this bitch would come through for a nigga and ended up with nothing.

When my phone vibrated in my hand, I anxiously answered it.

"Where the fuck are you?"

"At the door, Rudeness. Open up."

Vicious hung up the phone, and I had to calm myself down before I strangled the only person that could get what I wanted right now. I took a deep breath and opened the door to the hotel room, and she burst right in. Dressed in a pair of silver, glitter jeans, a see-through white top and a shaggy hot pink fur, Vicious looked like she was about to attend the fucking VMA's instead of an impromptu meeting.

She brushed past me and hurried towards the TV, switching it on.

"The remote! Where's the remote?"

"Fuck you yelling for?" I pointed in its direction as I watched her shuffle around like a chicken with her head cut off. "It's on the damn bed."

She grabbed the remote and then went back to stand in front of the TV. Once it was illuminated, she began flipping through channels quickly and after a few minutes, she landed on the one she wanted. There was a commercial on so she turned to face me with an exasperated look on her face.

"What?"

"What! What the fuck you mean, what?"

In less than a second, I was on her ass. I was already tired of her smart-ass mouth especially since she had yet to come through for a brotha. I wrapped my hands around her neck and squeezed, hoping to help her shut the hell up.

"Where is Kimani! You've had ample time to get that nigga and yet..."

My words were cut short when she slammed her hand down on my wrist, taking me by surprise and causing me to let go of the grip I had on her neck. Without warning, her knee collided with my dick, and I doubled over in pain. I looked up and saw her holding her neck and gasping for air all while shooting daggers at me.

"Don't put your fucking hands on me like you're crazy! I don't fucking play that shit!" she yelled through her coughs.

"Bitch…"

"Call me one more and I swear I will cut off your nut sack and use them as stress balls. Nigga, try me if you want to."

I struggled to my feet, grabbing the wall on my way up. This bitch was crazy. Talking about cutting my balls off. I walked over to the couch and took a seat, still holding my wounded dick.

"What the fuck you come over here acting crazy for?" I grumbled.

"Oh, you'll see. Just give it a second."

She turned her attention back to towards the TV where the news had just come back on. The blond white lady in the stiff suit started talking about breaking news, and an irritated scowl took over my face.

"More on our breaking news story. Top Record label executive known to the entertainment industry as Problem, was beaten and tortured within an inch of his life and found in his downtown L.A. condo early this morning. It is being reported that he sustained multiple stab wounds to his upper body, a severe head injury and the most gruesome of them all, his right arm had been completely skinned. We will continue to update you as more details come to light."

"What the fuck!" she screamed while pointing to the TV.

I shrugged. "I told you I would get you out of your contract. Done."

"You're really missing some screws."

"So I've been told. Look, is that all you came over here for?"

She stood to her feet, her anger obvious.

"Are you seriously trying to brush this off like you didn't skin a man like Hannibal Lector?"

I rolled my eyes. "Hannibal ate people, bruh."

"Minor details! Look, I wanted out of this contract but not like this. You're sick! And I'm done."

She grabbed her purse that had fallen from the crook of her arm and stormed towards the door. I quickly cut off her path and held out my arm to keep her from approaching the door.

"Where the fuck you think you going? I honored my end of the deal. After a little prodding and encouragement, Problem signed the papers that let you out of your contract. So, now it's your turn to pay up."

"What part of I'm not fucking with you do you not understand? When I agreed to this, I wasn't stupid. I know that you aren't some Hollywood agent like you pretended to be but I was desperate to get out of my contract. I thought maybe Problem needed a little strong arming, but this...this is just insane. I don't want to be associated with this in any way, shape or form. I'm out."

Before she could blink, I had my hand wrapped around her neck again, the gun that had been on my hip was now resting against her forehead. I cocked it back, and she flinched, closing her eyes tight.

"Listen to me and listen to me good. I'm not about to play with your dingy ass. The shit I did to him will be a walk in the park compared to what I'll do to you if you don't bring me Kimani. You have 24 hours or I'll pull out them dentures with pliers and snip off each one of your fingers like I'm pruning plants." I released the hold that I had on her, and she fell to the ground, wheezing. "24 hours, Vicious or they'll be reporting your death all over TMZ."

Vicious slowly rose from the floor and gathered herself. The fear in her eyes was clear; she was scared for her life. As she timidly walked out of the hotel room, I prayed that she was smart enough to do as she was told. I had zero patience left so if I had to deal with Vicious, my rage was probably going to make it hard to identify with her body. I was blood hungry, and if I couldn't get Kimani, she would take his place.

Kimani
September 2015

"The voicemail of the person that you are trying to reach is full."

"What the fuck, bro?" I mumbled as I ended the call.

I knew this nigga was still mad at me but damn. It had been impossible to get in touch with Grey for the last few days, and I just wanted to make sure he was good. Sighing out my frustration, I set my phone on the bed and took a seat on the edge.

"Where yo yellow ass at?"

I heard her before I saw her and I just shook my head. I already knew when I saw Blu that this shit wasn't going to be pleasant, but she was already on ten before she could get in the house good. Fuck man.

"I'm in the bedroom, B. And lower your damn voice."

She appeared in the doorway a few seconds later and even though her face was balled up in anger, my dick still got hard at the sight of her. She was fucking gorgeous and even sexier when she was mad. It was going to be extremely hard to focus on whatever the hell she was mad at because all I could think about was getting up in her guts.

"Lower my voice? Are you serious right now? You out all damn night and then call me with some female in the background, and you don't think that I deserve to fucking raise my voice?!" she screamed.

"Blu, look. That shit ain't even what you thinking it is."

"Oh no?" She reached down in her purse and pulled out her phone. She started to scroll through it, searching for something before she turned the screen towards me. "You weren't out with your ex-girlfriend? You didn't get in her car? You didn't go to her house? She didn't bring you fucking bagels after you dicked her down?" Her voice had elevated to a pitch only dogs could hear.

I got off the bed and smacked her phone across the room. I didn't even have to look at it to know that it was some damn gossip blog that had reported me leaving the club with Vicious. Those damn reporters were a pain in my ass.

"I know you don't remember much about me, but I can assure you I'm not that nigga. One thing I don't do is this loud arguing shit. You got something you want to discuss; you can talk to me like an adult." I brushed past her and out of the bedroom.

Blu was hot on my heels as I made my way to the kitchen to grab a drink. After last night's bullshit, I should have been done with alcohol for a while but her attitude was pissing me off, and I needed something to take the edge off before I hurt her ass.

"You got hella nerve! You all over the fucking blogs and shit prancing around with your thotty ex and you want me to talk to you like an adult?"

I walked over to the bar and poured myself a double shot of Hennessey. Throwing them back, I welcomed the slight burn in my throat before I turned my attention back towards my screaming girlfriend.

"Yeah, once you pass the age of 17, you become one of those. Or did you forget how to be an adult too?"

I knew that I had hit her with a low blow once I saw her eye twitch. It only happened when she was either extremely hurt or upset...and I was sure that she was both right now.

"Nah, I didn't forget that, but you must've forgotten who you're dealing with. You're right about me not remembering much about you, but I remember everything about me. I know that I was fine before you came along and I'll be good after you. Which starts now."

With tears pooling in her eyes, Blu stormed away from me and back into the bedroom. Shit. This was not where this discussion was supposed to go. I had spent almost a year without Blu in my life, thinking that she was dead, and my soul had ached the entire time. And now, because of my mouth and Vicious' schemin' ass, I was about to lose her again. I quickly poured myself another shot and took it to the head before I headed for my bedroom. When I got there, Blu was grabbing all of her toiletries from the bathroom and throwing them in her suitcase. She didn't pay a nigga no mind as she tried to brush past me but I caught her arm and held her in place.

"Blu, man. I'm sorry."

"Well, that's something we can both agree on. But whatever man. It's not like I remember you anyway, right?"

I sighed. "I apologize, B. That shit was below the belt and uncalled for. But you wouldn't even let a nigga explain."

Blu snatched away from me and folded her arms against her chest.

"Explain what? Where would you even start? Are you going to explain why you were photographed hanging with the ex you claim to hate? Or why you were at her house this morning? Or better yet are you going to explain why you haven't been here at all? Why you haven't even made an effort to talk to me about anything that's happened or what we are even doing?"

Tears had sprung from her eyes, and her body began to tremble. I started to say something, but she held her hand up to silence me before she continued.

"I've been gone for a whole year. My entire memory of you has disappeared into thin air. And you haven't even sat down to ask me how I feel! I'm here alone every damn day trying to sort out my thoughts and figure out what's what, and you don't even care! You can try and pull some excuse from your ass, but you've been avoiding me like the plague because you don't want to deal with it. Well, don't even worry about it. You don't have to deal with it, me or *us* anymore."

She stormed into the bathroom, slamming the door. I can't lie, the shit she was saying was on point. I hadn't even admitted it to myself, but I had been avoiding dealing with the issue of Blu's memory loss because it fucked with me. I had loved her so damn hard. The shit that I felt for her was life-altering and soul-stirring. But the truth was that it fucked with me to know that she couldn't remember anything that I had felt for her, said to her, done with her or *for* her. What was I supposed to do with that? How was I supposed to get her past that point? What if she re-learned me and she wasn't fucking with a nigga? What if we missed our window? What if that once in a lifetime thing we had was only for that moment? They say lightning never strikes twice in the same place, and a nigga was terrified that that shit would ring true for our relationship. I was positive that I wouldn't be able to handle her leaving me again.

So I had subconsciously been avoiding her. I had been burying myself in work and Grey's drama to avoid having to deal with the fallout of what had happened to her. Hearing her become emotional behind my actions had me messed up in the head, but on the real I didn't even know what to say to her. I just knew that I couldn't let her leave me. So I approached the bathroom door and knocked lightly. She didn't respond, but I could hear her sniffling.

"Blu, baby, a nigga sorry, ok? I mean real deal sorry from the bottom of my heart and shit. Please just come out so that we can talk. Please?"

I waited for a few minutes, but Blu didn't respond. That was okay because this time I wasn't running. I turned around and sat on the bed, my head buried in my hands. I would wait out here all night if I had too. Running my hands over my hair, I sighed deeply. Getting comfortable in the bed, I waited for her to come out the bathroom so that I could make things right.

The sound of a horn honking jarred me out of my sleep. I hadn't even realized that I'd fallen asleep until I was awakened. I looked in the direction of the bathroom, and my heart sank. The door was open, and her suitcase was gone. I had been so busy running that I hadn't even noticed that I had pushed Blu to lace up *her* track shoes. Damn.

Blaze
September 2015

I opened my eyes and they darted around the room only for my heart to be filled with disappointment. This was the second day that I had been awake from my coma and still hadn't seen Grey's face. To say that my heart was breaking a little bit with each passing second would be an understatement. I didn't understand why he wasn't here. Yes, I knew that he was probably busying himself with trying to find the people who did this, but the nurses had told me that he hadn't been here but once since I was admitted and he had refused to come into the room. I could understand that it may have been hard for him to see me in this condition, but that shit was extremely selfish. I fought back the tears as I heard the doorknob turn to my room.

Amber, my nurse, walked in with a bright smile on her face. Even though I was beyond pissed, I couldn't help but smile back at her. She was so bubbly and sweet. She let me have visitors past the visiting hours, and she went above and beyond to do her job. I was extremely grateful that she had been assigned to me.

"Good morning, Blaze! How are you feeling today?" She set her iPad down on the chair and went to check my monitors.

"I'm okay, I guess."

"We'll I've got some good news for you."

I pushed myself to sit up straighter in the bed, wincing in pain the entire time.

"Yeah? What's that?"

"You're being released today!" she said in a sing-song voice.

"Released? Why? Uh, didn't I just wake up from a coma? Ya'll don't think I need to stay here a little longer?"

Amber laughed as she reached for her iPad and opened up my medical charts. "Well, it seems as if your fiancée is anxious for you to be home. He's arranged for a private doctor to take care of you in your home until your condition improves. So as soon as I update your charts and get them over to your new doctor, you'll be free to go!"

"Is my fiancée picking me up?"

"Umm, I'm not sure. Let me check with Raina really quick."

She offered me a small smile and exited the room but returned a few minutes later.

"He ordered a car service for you."

I saw the sympathy in her eyes, and I immediately became embarrassed. Refusing to let it show, I smiled, hoping that it reached my eyes.

"Ok cool. Hopefully, they'll stop at In-and-Out on the way. I've only had cafeteria food for one day, and I'm already over it."

Amber laughed and helped me get ready to leave the hospital. An hour later I was dressed in the Adidas track suit that Grey had sent over and a pair of shell toes. Amber had assisted me in pulling the ridiculousness that was on my head back into a decent bun and had even helped me apply a bit of makeup. Even though I was good and pissed with Grey, I still didn't want to look like who done it and what for when he saw me.

After placing me in a wheelchair, Amber rolled me down to the lobby, and we waited for the car. A few minutes later a black medical transport van pulled up, and the driver hopped out to help me in. I said my goodbyes to Amber before the door closed. I wasn't sure what kind of van we were in, but as soon as we pulled out of the parking lot, my ass was knocked out.

The deep grumble of a male voice pulled me out of the deep sleep. "Let's go."

I lazily opened my eyes, checked out my surroundings, and the first thing that I noticed was that it was pitch black outside. When we left the hospital, it was only a little past noon. The drive from the hospital to Grey's house was less than fifteen minutes so the fact that it was as dark as it was, alarmed the hell out of me. The second thing I noticed was that we were in front of a large-ass house that looked nothing like Grey's...where I was *supposed* to be. Even though the house was large and looked like it could have once been a real estate gem, it now looked like something out of a horror movie.

"Let's go," the man repeated.

I could hear my heart beating in my ears, and my breath grew sharp instantly. I shook my head and backed up into the car as far away from him as I possibly go, but he hopped in and dragged me out. The pain from the healing gunshot wound radiated through my whole body as he roughly tossed me over his shoulder and carried me to the house. Screaming, yelling, and kicking was all I was doing. The driver carried on like this shit I was doing didn't faze him in the least bit. He walked onto the large front porch and opened the front door, dropping me on my ass once we were inside. I groaned as my body hit the floor sending waves of pain through every bone in my body. As I tried to stand, I saw something that literally knocked the wind out of me.

Standing at the foot of the long spiral staircase was my father, Baron, and Grey's ex-fiancé, Nakami. Although seeing Baron came as a bit of a shock, I was more than surprised to see Nakami's ass. Grey hadn't come out and told me that he'd killed her but when she went missing, I assumed, along with everyone else, that she was dead. But apparently Grey hadn't tied up all his loose ends like he had suggested. Nakami read the confusion on my face and smiled sinisterly. Baron spread his arms just as wide as the grin on his face before he spoke.

"Welcome home, Cadence."

Blu
September 2015

I slid my glass towards the bartender. "A double shot this time, please." She nodded her head before grabbing my glass and walking away.

I had been sitting at the hotel bar for an hour trying to get my emotions in check. They were all over the place after the argument that I'd had with Kimani, and I wasn't sure what I even wanted to do. My mind was telling me to get on somebody's plane and get far the fuck away from California, but my heart was telling me to stay. I knew that I was on some bullshit leaving while Kimani was sleep and shit but I just knew that he was going to try and sweet talk me or sex me out of my feelings, and that's not what I needed. What I needed was some time and some space to figure things out. So I had retreated to a hotel and ended up at the bar, drinking my problems away.

I was tempted to call Marquis or Tatum, but when I said I needed space, I meant from everyone. As great as it would have been to talk this out with them, I didn't need their opinions swaying the way that I felt. I just needed to be able to make up my own mind. The bartender came back with my double shot, and I immediately tossed it back, wincing as

the room temperature liquid coursed down my throat. I
knew that at this point if I was to have any more liquor,
someone would be carrying me back to my room, so I closed
out my tab and headed for the elevator. The entire ride to
my floor, I could feel the liquor taking effect, and I enjoyed
being able to escape my worries if only for a moment. I
swayed back and forth as a seemingly random Beyoncé song
filled my head.

I, feel weak. We've been here before.
Cause I, feel we, keep going back and forth
Maybe it's over, maybe we're through
But I honestly can say, I still love you
And maybe we've reached the mountain peak
And there's nowhere left to climb
And maybe we lost the magic piece
And we're both too blind to find
Let's start over, let's give love their wings
Let's start over, stop fighting bout the same ol' things
Let's start over, we can't let our good love die
Maybe we can start all over, give love another life.

By the time I had finished whisper-singing the
emotional song, the elevator doors had sprung open and so

had the floodgates. Tears were streaming down my face in at a maddening pace, and my heart felt like it was being shredded into tiny pieces. I knew that I loved Kimani; it was something that I felt in every fiber of my being. But I was not about to sit around and wait for him to stop being scared to deal with what I...what *we* had been through. I had been through enough, and the last thing I needed was to be neglected. I stepped off the elevator trying to collect myself. My eyes were pointed towards the ground in an attempt to dry them with my hands. Right before I reached my door, I slammed into a muscular body and instead of hitting the ground due to the impact of the collision, I landed in the person's arms.

"You know I hate to see you cry."

The sound of his voice scared me, and I hurried to get out of his grasp. I backed myself into a wall trying to figure out how he had found me again. Israel stood on the other side of the hallway, staring at me intensely, as though he was trying to figure out what to say next.

"Are you fucking stalking me, Israel?" I asked, beating him to the punch.

"I...no...I'm just..." his voice trailed off as he looked down at the ground.

I watched him closely, my fear starting to fade. He looked like a lost child and not the ruthless kidnapper that he had been made out to be. He cleared his throat and spoke, finally finding his words. "I just wanted to make sure that you were okay."

"Why wouldn't I be? I'm back where I belong," I said with attitude.

Israel looked around confused. "At a hotel?"

"With Kimani, dumbass."

"Don't look like you're with him now. Looks like ya'll got into it and you retreated to a hotel."

I rolled my eyes. Forcing myself off the wall, I dug the room key out of my pocket and approached the door. "Whatever the case, none of what I do is any of your concern. You lost that right when I found out that you're a fucking kidnapper. So how about you leave me alone and go find your next victim."

I stuck the key card in the slot on the door and pushed the handle downward. Before I could get the door fully open to walk through, Israel had his hand up, blocking my way inside.

"Damn, is that how you really feel about me, Blu?"

The sadness in his eyes couldn't be missed. My words had struck a nerve and the pain that they had caused radiated off of him. I felt bad.

"That was uncalled for. I'm sor—"

"Don't even worry about it, B." He shook his head and started to walk off.

I don't know if it was the obvious regret that was all up in his body language or the liquor coursing through my body and affecting my brain cells, but before I could stop myself, I called out to him. He turned around and waited for me to say something. Not knowing what else so say, I invited him in my room.

"Uh, you sure?" he asked.

"No, but is that going to stop you from coming in? C'mon before I realize what I'm doing and I change my mind."

I pushed the door open and waited for him to follow behind me. Once he was inside the room, I let the door close and stepped out of my heels, tossing them against the wall. Israel took a seat on the couch on the far side of the room, and I stood at the window, taking in the view of Downtown L.A. The room fell silent for a while, both of us wrapped up in our thoughts. After a few minutes, it was Israel who finally spoke up.

"I know what you think of me. And I can't even be mad that it's how you feel. I did some unforgivable shit trying to make some shit right that would never be right, and now we're here. I'm in love with your ass, and you can barely stand the sight of me."

"Why? Why'd you do this to me?" I asked him. As tired as I was of crying, tears still pooled in my eyes as I thought about what he'd taken away from me.

"I thought...I thought that my brother was right. I thought that the niggas that killed my father and put my sister in a coma needed to fucking die. Why should they live when my family was torn to pieces because they couldn't take the fucking heat? When this shit started, I wanted the same thing my brother did—revenge."

I watched as Israel stood from the couch and paced the floor.

"Giving you those pills...I ain't even gon' lie. That shit was fucked up. I don't ever think I can apologize enough for what I did. I didn't plan to fall in love with you like I did. It was so fucking easy to do that I didn't realize how I felt until you walked away. But when you left, that shit nearly killed me. Nothing else mattered in that moment other than getting you back. Not Grey, not Kimani, not my father. Not

Roman. I told him that I was done with his bullshit because all I wanted out of life was you."

Israel slowed his pace and started walking towards me. My heart rate sped up; not because I was fearful of what he might do but because he was making me feel...something.

"I believed my own hype for the longest. I honestly thought that I was that good of a damn actor." He chuckled to himself, then took my hand and placed it on his heart, which was beating furiously. "But you...you got in here, Blu."

As easy as it would have been to dismiss his words as a ploy to use me in him and his brother's twisted game of revenge, I knew the moment my hand landed on his chest, that he was dead ass serious. He loved me. He was going against everything that his brother had planned. His only family. He was willing to destroy his relationship with his brother just to have me. Which was more than I could say about Kimani.

Where Kimani was trying to avoid dealing with the hard shit, Israel was willing to confront the issue head on. Where Kimani refused to sacrifice *anything* in order to sort things out, Israel was giving up everything—in order to be with me. I *wanted* to walk to the door and show Israel out. I *wanted* to thank him for his apology, forgive him and close the door to that chapter of my life. But I didn't do any of those things. Instead, I stood on my tiptoes so that I could reach Israel's face, grabbed the back of his head and smashed his lips against mine.

It was probably a mix of the liquor and the confession he'd made, but I felt something for him. I wasn't sure that it was love. At least not the level of love that I could tell that he had for me or the level of love that I had for Kimani, but it was something. And all I needed in that moment was *something.* He kissed me back, transferring an immeasurable amount of passion. I was positive that he could tell hadn't been returned on my end, but we kept going. Israel's hands grabbed at my body, molding and kneading me like I was a lump of clay. Being touched, being needed, being wanted...felt so damn good. I moaned into his mouth as his hands pushed the fabric of my light jersey dress up my thighs and over my ass, exposing my cheeks.

Israel bit down on my bottom lip while swiping his tongue across my top lip and his hand roamed the cracked of my ass. Annoyed with the fabric of my dress standing in the way, Israel used his left hand to yank the body of the dress from its thin spaghetti straps, causing my titties to bounce free. He groaned at the sight of them and anxiously broke our kisses to tend to my hardened nipples. As soon as his tongue made contact with them, my head fell back in ecstasy. With his hand at the small of my back, Israel kneeled down and pinched my nipple between his teeth and then extended his jaw in small in-and-out motions. My whole body prickled with goosebumps. As he worked my breasts, I reached into the black sweatpants he was wearing and grabbed ahold of his thick, rock solid dick and began to stroke it. Whenever I felt his tongue swirl around one of my nipples, I let one of my fingers swipe the tip of his dick where pre-cum was starting to ooze out.

Suddenly, Israel pushed me away and stood all the way up. He stepped out of his pants as I shrugged what was left of my dress off my shoulders. As I stood there watching him snatch his shirt over his head, I still wasn't sure of what I was about to do, but I knew that It was too late to back out now. I had crossed the line, and I didn't feel that bad about it. I needed to feel something reciprocal. I had gone too many weeks trying to get a man to show me what he told me he felt, and I was damn tired of being neglected. Even though in my heart I knew that Israel was the wrong man, he was making me feel like I mattered. And that's all that I wanted. I wasn't concerned about the fallout; I just wanted to feel loved.

After he put on a condom, he scooped me up in his arms and carried me over to the window as I wrapped my legs around his torso, our lips reconnecting like long lost lovers. Lifting me up slighting, he positioned himself at my opening and slowly slid inside, his girth causing me to inhale sharply.

"Fuck, Blu," Israel hissed my ear.

Against the window with the beautiful view behind me, Israel proceeded to sex me down. He paid attention to every single, solitary spot on my body, making me cum multiple times; the magnitude of each orgasm differing. He took his time pleasing me, making sure that I spent all of my energy and rewarding me with pleasure with his every stroke. He was tender and sweet at some points and rough and unapologetically deep at others. He gave all of himself to me, trying to prove that his love for me was real. And I was convinced.

But it wasn't enough. After every stroke, every thrust, every moan, every orgasm, I thought of Kimani. I wished for *him* to be the one running his hands up and down my body. I wanted *him* to be the one whispering my name and touching the centermost part of me. It felt great to have someone show me just how deeply they felt about me, but it was the wrong person. I felt it the entire time and by the time we finished, I was positive that Israel could feel it too. Kimani was all up and through my veins, and I couldn't shake him. He was all that I wanted. I felt horrible for being with Israel knowing that my heart belonged to Kimani, but I was vulnerable and drunk, and Israel was saying everything that I wanted Kimani to say. What was done was done. I just hoped that I could deal with the consequences.

Kimani

September 2015

"Who the fuck is banging at my damn door like they the boys?"

Tossing the blanket that lay haphazardly on my body, I got up from the couch and made my way to the door. Since Blu had left a few hours ago, I had tried to fall back to sleep, but she invaded my thoughts every time I closed my eyes. I was butt hurt, man. I needed Blu back in my life like I needed oxygen. I didn't know where she had gone or how to find her, but I knew that I wasn't going to wait more than another hour or two for her to change her mind and come back home to a nigga. If she wasn't back to the crib soon, a nigga was putting out an APB on her ass. I approached the door and took a deep breath before I swung it open.

"You gotta be fucking shitting me, I groaned.

I had just had the day from hell, and the last person that I wanted to see was the one standing on the other side of my door. With a worried expression on her face, Vicious stepped over the threshold, looking around corners and shit.

"Vicious, what are you doing here? And what the hell are you looking for?"

I grabbed at her arm, pulling her back to me. She looked at me with wide, fearful eyes. That was something new because the Vicious I was familiar with wasn't scared of a damn thing and she most definitely wasn't scared of the kid.

She grabbed my face in her hands, inspecting it like a mother would a child. "Are you ok? Nothing happened did it? Nobody's been here?"

I knocked her hands away and held her away from my body.

"I'm fine. Now answer my question. What the fuck are you doing here?"

"I'm sorry, Kimani. I'm sorry! I didn't mean to get you involved in this shit! I was just desperate to get out of it. I'm so sorry!" Vicious ranted while tears streamed down her face.

I was confused as fuck. What the hell was she apologizing for? I needed her to calm down because she was so upset that she was talking hella fast, and everything that was coming out of her mouth sounded like a foreign language. I grabbed ahold of her arm and shook her a little, in effort to get her to calm down. But instead of getting herself together, she let out a bloodcurdling scream as she cast her gaze on something behind me. I attempted to turn around to figure out what had her so shook but before I could, I was hit hard on the head, and it was lights out for your boy.

Grey
September 2015

"Fuck, Kimani! Pick up your fucking phone!" I screamed.

The shit that Nine had told me on the phone had me regretting each and every time that I had sent her to voicemail over the last few weeks. When she dropped the bomb on me that Nakami's nutty ass had survived her gunshot wounds and the fucking fire, I damn near lit that whole hotel I was staying in on fire. Then she had the nerve to further fuck my mind up by telling me that she was Nakami's ol' lady and that Nakami had been working with Roman to get at me the entire time. The shit blew me. I knew that I had dope dick, but for real for real, no broad should ever be that crazy over a nigga.

Yeah, I know that I had offed her father and claimed his empire as my own, but I had the feeling that Nakami's main motivation for revenge was because a nigga just wasn't trying to put up with her lunatic ass. After Nine dropped that information on me, I checked out the hotel and hit up Gertrude to see if Harmony could stay with them for a week or so while I handled the situation at home. She quickly agreed, and I hopped my ass on the jet to get back to Cali. There was no telling what a mind as twisted as Nakami's had come up with and I was praying that she hadn't harmed my brother or Blaze.

Imagine my fucking surprise when I called the got damn hospital to find out that not only had Blaze awakened up from her coma but that she had been discharged and taken to a private doctor that I had arranged and cleared with the hospital. I had lit the fuck into Mizhani after that because she was supposed to be my eyes and ears at the hospital. She apologized profusely, stating that she had an issue at one of the traps that caused her to run late and by the time she got to the hospital, they told her the same thing she'd told me. I was fucking pissed but more at myself than her. It had Nakami written all over it. My only hope was that that stupid bitch was keeping Blaze alive so that she could use her as a bargaining tool to get to me. If she had harmed Blaze in any way, shape or form, I was going to get Charles Manson scary out this bitch and kill everything moving.

I had just landed ten minutes ago and had been trying feverishly to get in touch with my brother, but his phone was going to voicemail. After trying him one more time, I called Blu hoping that she was with him.

"Hello?"

"Blu, where's my brother?"

"I...I... I don't know," she stuttered.

"Bitch I don't have time for you to be Stuttering Stanley. Tell me what the fuck you know!"

"Grey, if he's not at home I don't know where he is. We got into an argument earlier, and I left. What is this about? Why are you---"

Cutting her off, I started, "That bitch Nakami is still alive. She—"

"Oh my fucking God!" she yelled, interrupting me. "I fucking forgot to tell him!"

"Tell him what?" I could hear her crying, but I could give a fuck less. "TELL HIM WHAT, BLU?!"

"I saw Nakami at the hospital today. She said that she was still looking for you and that basically she would hurt anyone that stood in her way...including me and Kimani. Oh my God! If something happens to him..."

I hung up the phone and wrapped my fingers around my phone as tight as they would go. Fury is probably the best way to describe what I was feeling. I liked Blu; I really did, but if her forgetting to mention the Nakami shit to my brother proved to be detrimental, I would light her up with bullets and not even blink. The fucked up part of all this is that I hadn't even spoken to my brother since he told me about him chopping it up with the Feds. I was still pissed at that situation because if nothing else, he should have come to me; but I loved that nigga, and I wouldn't know what to do if I lost him.

I stood on the tarmac contemplating my next move. With Blaze and Kimani missing, I hadn't the slightest clue where the hell to ever start looking for them. All I knew was that I wasn't going to be able to do this shit by myself. After I calmed down the best that I could, I called Brandin and put him up on game.

"Shit, man. Aight," Brandin said. "So I'll get Cope, Treach and Keem to go over to Kimani's place. See if we can get some information off his security shit. I know he got cameras and shit, right?"

"Yeah, yeah. When I had my security system put in, I had his done too. Aight cool."

"Bet. Me, Mihzani, Seven and Jah gon' split up. I'ma have Mihzani and Seven check out the hospital and see what kind of info they can get about Blaze's bogus discharge and me and Jah gon run up in every spot Nakami used to be at. We gon' find them, bruh. Believe that."

"Fa'sho man. Let me know."

I hung up feeling a little better about the situation but still stressed out. Another minute or two rolled by and my whip rolled up. The valet driver got out, and I tossed him a buck fifty before easing into my ride and taking off. Before I could get my thoughts together, my phone rang. I didn't bother taking my eyes off the road to look at the caller; I just turned on the Bluetooth in the car and answered.

"What?"

"Is that how you address your former fiancé?" Nakami's voice floated through the speakers of my car immediately causing my face to flush with anger.

"It is when that bitch is fuckin' crazy, and you have a *new* fiancé that sucks the dick better. What the fuck you want, hoe? I hate that your ass survived death, but I'm letting you know now, you ain't like ya motha. You ain't got nine lives."

"Fuck that bitch and fuck you. I suggest that you change your attitude, or I'll have to put a bullet through Blaze's big ass earlier than I planned."

The mention of Blaze's name caused me to swerve. *So that nut job does have her.* Getting myself together before I got pulled over by the boys, I pulled back in my lane and hit cruise control.

"You bluffing. You ain't got my baby," I said calmly. I needed proof that Blaze was there and alive.

She sucked her teeth. "Blaze will do just fine when you're addressing her."

"Oh, word? Let me find out you jealous of my soulmate, Nakami. That shit ain't a good look, ma." I said, taunting her.

"KARMA!" she screamed. "My name is Karma, nigga! KARMA!"

"I don't give a fuck what your name is. The only thing I'm going to be calling you is dead."

"Baby, please. Just do what she says! This bitch is crazy!" I heard Blaze's sweet voice pouring through the speakers, and I had to show major restraint.

Confirming that she was with Nakami fucked me up because there was no telling what her demented ass had in mind. Fuck all this playing around on the phone. I needed to get to B.

"You got my brother too, bitch?" I yelled.

"Your brother? Why do I need him when I have someone so much better? Look I'm tired of playing on the phone with you. You need to bring two million in cash to the address I'm about to text you. You have two hours to get here. No guns, no funny shit, and no pigs. Or baby girl eats a bullet. You feel me?"

"I ain't got two million just fucking laying around!"

"Damn, Blaze. I'd hate to break it to you, but it sounds like your little fiancé doesn't value your life like you think he does. Or else he wouldn't be sitting on the fucking phone

TRYING TO PLAY ME! Nigga, you're the plug! You made sure of that, didn't you? So don't insult my muthafucking intelligence by telling me you don't have the money. Since you want to act brand new, the amount is now *three million,* and you have *two* hours. Play with me if you want."

The line went dead, and I slammed my hands on the dash hard.

"FUCK!" I shouted.

Although I was glad that I had some more information about Blaze's whereabouts, I was still vexed about where Kimani was. Until I got more information from Brandin or Cope, Blaze was my immediate concern. I made a quick u-turn and headed back into the direction of my office where my safe was. I needed to get the money and get to Blaze. As soon as I hit the freeway, my line rang again. I hit accept on my dash screen and answered in irritation.

"The fuck you want now, Nakami? Or Karma. Whatever the hell you're going by."

He laughed. "This ain't no fucking Karma. Well, I guess in a way it is."

I had never heard his voice before but I quickly assumed I was talking to one of my brothers. One of my *other* brothers.

"Which coward is this? Roman or Israel?"

"The only coward on this phone is you, pussy. But we'll save that discussion for later."

"Ain't no later, nigga! Say what you need to say now!"

"Grey man, I'm good. Don't come for me. It's my fault. I'll take the hit man."

"No, no, no, no!" I could feel the tears forming in my eyes at the sound of Kimani's voice but now was not the time for pussy nigga tears.

"It doesn't feel good to know that you're about to lose someone you're close to does it? At least you have a heads up. But I tell you what. I'm going to give you a chance to say goodbye to your brother in person."

"Don't do it, Grey! Fuck him!" Kimani shouted in the background.

"Shut up!" Roman roared.

"Mannn, fuck you!" Kimani responded.

A gun went off, and I could feel my heart drop like an elevator. More commotion sounded in the background before that nigga returned to the phone.

"My bad. For a little pansy ass model nigga, he sure has a lot of heart. What was I saying? Oh yeah, I was being a nice ass nigga and letting you say your final goodbyes to your brother. One hour, nigga. I'm plugging the address into your GPS favorites."

"You what?"

"Oh, yeah nigga I hacked your phone. Once we get off the line, all your phone features will be disabled except for the GPS. No email, Facetime, iMessage…none of that. And don't even bother with your office and house. That shit been disabled too. Just bring your ass to the spot. I shouldn't have to tell you what'll happen if you don't show, right?"

His laugh was the last thing I heard before the line went dead. Hurriedly, I picked up my phone from the passenger seat and tried to dial Brandin but sure enough, my email, phone and messages had been disabled. FUCK! Nakami had Blaze, and one of my brothers had Kimani. I only had the time and resources to save one of them. I couldn't think of anything worse than the predicament that I was in. What the fuck was a nigga to do?

Blu
September 2015

I couldn't stop the heavy stream of tears from coating my face. I was past distraught; I was downright terrified. Being selfish, I might have inadvertently put Kimani in harm's way. Not only did I just fuck another man—a man that had kidnapped and erased the memories of the man that I loved, but I had forgotten to tell him about crucial information that could have saved his life. If something happened to Kimani because I had neglected to tell him about Kimani, I would never forgive myself.

Israel sat next to me on the bed, rubbing my back as I cried harder than I ever remember crying before. Grey was pissed and rightfully so, and I had no idea how to help. I wanted to do something to make up for everything but what could I do? I was just a former stripper who gave up on love too easily and fell into the enemy's arms.

"What if....What if something happens to him?" I choked out. I was having a Kim Kardashian ugly cry moment if there ever was one.

Israel remained quiet, his repetitive hand movement on my back slowing down as the minutes ticked away. Nothing but the sound of my sobs filled the air until he cleared his throat and spoke.

"You really love him, huh?" he asked.

I looked at him through my sheet of tears, and his pain reflected mine. My soul was hurting at the possibility of me causing Kimani pain, and his was hurting because he knew that there was no more hope for us.

"More than life. I don't even know him, but I feel it in my bones. In my soul. In my heart. He loved me when I wasn't sure if I loved myself. He... he..."

Just speaking on the love I felt for Kimani caused more tears to erupt from my body. I should have been patient! I should have communicated! But now I was sitting here making myself physically and emotionally sick because I had been too quick to react. My leg started to vibrate, and I looked down to see Israel's phone going off beside me. Roman's name lit up the screen, and he picked it up, telling me to stay quiet.

"Yo."

"Where you at, nigga? I need your help."

Roman's voice bounced off the walls of the hotel room once Israel placed him on speaker.

"I told you I was done, bro. I meant that shit."

"You so knee deep in that bitch pussy that you gon say fuck your blood, nigga?"

I hopped up off the bed ready to rip Roman a new asshole, but Israel placed his finger to his lips, signaling for me to stay quiet.

"It is what it is. You too gone off this revenge shit. You need to let that shit ride."

"Too fucking late for that now," he grunted.

"What you mean by that?"

Silence followed Israel's question.

"Ro! What the fuck you mean by that, nigga?"

Roman huffed. "I got his brother."

My heart plummeted to the lobby of the hotel after hearing him say that. I started to open my mouth, but before I could get words out, Israel had his hand up against it, forcing me to stay silent.

"You what?"

"I ain't stutter, fool. I got his brother, and I'm about to have him too. He's coming to me thinking that he's going to be able to say his final goodbyes to his pretty boy ass brother, but he'll be dead way before he gets there.

Angry tears rushed from my eyes coated Israel's fingers. I had been worried about Nakami and had quickly forgotten about the other person that was gunning for their family. I felt the urge to throw up, but I swallowed hard so that I could finish listening to the rest of their conversation.

"Aight, aight. Uh, where you at? I'ma come thru and help you."

"Oh, now you want to help now that I told you that I did all the hard parts."

"Nigga, you want me to help or nah? I don't have a problem staying out of this shit and letting you off that nigga. Shit, it might benefit me more if that nigga was out the picture anyway."

I shot Israel a glare that would have sent him straight to hell if it had the ability to kill. He looked at me with pleading eyes, silently begging me to chill.

"Okay, okay. I'ma text you the address. Hurry up, though; I only gave him one hour, so you got less than that to get here."

The phone hung up, and I pushed Israel's hand away from my body. With no warning, I started raining blows on him as hard as I could. I knew that I had fucked up his mental by having sex with him and then turning around and professing my love to another nigga, but discussing with his brother how he wanted to help murder the man I loved was just cruel.

"You fucking bastard! Why would you do this! I hate you!" I screamed while hitting with all the force I could muster.

Israel grabbed my wrists and held me away from his body with an irritated look on his face.

"Yo, chill Ali! I'm not helping him kill nobody. I'm going to stop him."

His phone lit up and showed the text that contained the address from Roman. Grabbing it, he placed it in his pocket and grabbed his keys off the couch.

"Wait!" I yelled after him. "I'm coming with you."

Karma
September 2015

The wait was killing me. I was wet with anticipation of seeing Grey up close and in person for the first time in almost a year. I was damn near salivating at the thought of looking into his grey eyes before I put a bullet between them. Killing him was definitely in the plans, but mama was going to have some fun first.

"I never knew you were this sick in the head. You seemed so fucking normal," Blaze muttered.

In one swift move, I was across the room and in her face; my hand colliding against her pretty brown skin with the force of a semi-truck. I damn near slapped the melanin off her. I bent down and got into her face.

"And I never knew that you were a homewrecker, you fat bitch. But keep talking slick and see if I don't have something *sick* for you while we wait for *our* man."

"Karma, what did that nigga say about the money? He's bringing the 1.5 mil, right?" Baron's voice boomed as he came into the room.

I rolled my eyes. I was so sick of this Fetty Wap, Captain Hook pirate patch looking ass nigga. I stared at him for a full second before I grabbed the gun from the table behind me and let off three rounds, hitting him in his stomach, chest and forehead. Blaze screamed loud and high, causing me to turn the gun her way.

"That was your pimp-daddy I just killed and you screaming like you just saw Jesus die on the cross. Shut that shit up before you're next," I growled.

I tucked the gun inside the waistband of my form-fitting camo pants and took a look around. Things were coming together so well I just had to pat myself on the back. I tried to warn Baron's dumb ass that trust was something that I didn't believe in, but he was so anxious to get this money, that he failed to heed my warning. I only needed him to help get Blaze out of the hospital and to the safe house. Now that she was here, I didn't need that worrisome ass nigga involved in my plans. Plus, once I killed Grey and his bitch, I was going to need that money to start my new life in Europe. Three million was not the kind of money I was used to having at my disposal, but it would have to do for now. I was sure that when I landed in Europe, my hustler's mentality would kick in and I could flip that three mil like a muthafucking pancake.

Blaze was handcuffed to the bed frame that had been nailed to the floor, so I went to freshen up before Grey arrived. I had plans for that nigga. I climbed the stairs and made my way to the second floor of the large estate and walked into the master bedroom. The body of the real estate agent that had shown me the property a few days ago still lay in the same spot she had died in and I just stepped over her like she wasn't there. She was starting to smell, but I didn't worry about it too much because, after today, I would be gone anyway. I opened my suitcase and rifled through it until I found the perfect thing to wear. Satisfied, I went into the adjoining bathroom and ran a shower. I hadn't gotten sweaty but I needed to be squeaky clean and smelling like fresh fruit before I saw Grey.

I stepped in the shower and a multitude of emotions consumed me. I had mixed emotions about Grey. On one hand, I hated him for the shit that had gone down with Blu and of course, for killing my father. But on the other hand, my heart still ached for him. I had loved him with my whole heart and I still desired him. He was everything, and I was sure that my feelings would multiply once I saw him in person. My body was already starting to react to just the thought of him. Reminding myself that I only had 40 minutes until he was set to arrive, I quickly lathered and rinsed my body, took care of my feminine hygiene and got out of the shower. Once inside the room, I lotioned my entire body and added a palm full of mousse to my wet hair.

I was going for a Beyonce's "Drunk in Love" vibe with the stringy wet bob look. Spritzing myself down in my Hypnotic Poison Eau de Toilelette by Dior, I got dressed humming along to Rihanna.

I was good on my own, that's the way it was, that's the way it was
You was good on the low for a faded fuck, on some faded love,
Shit, what the fuck you complaining for, feeling jaded huh?
Used to trip off that shit I was kicking to you,
Had some fun on the run, boy I'll give it to you
But baby, don't get it twisted
You was just another nigga on the hit list
Tryna fix your inner issues with a bad bitch
Didn't they tell you that I was a savage
Fuck ya white horse and a carriage
Bet you never could imagine
Never told you could have it
But you needed me...

I smiled as I fixed myself in the mirror. Tonight was the night that I finally got what I wanted. The excitement made my skin tingle and my pussy throb. I was ready and I only hoped that this would be the night everything ended.

Grey
September 2015

I pulled up and put the car in park once my GPS told me that I had reached my final destination. I was a nigga that was never scared of anything. No man or woman on earth could shake me, but having to make a choice like this had a nigga nervous. I was taking a risk, and I was hoping that it paid off. Grabbing the duffle bag from the backseat, I got out of the car. Stepping up to the door, I started to knock but before I could, the door swung open, and I was greeted by the strangest sight. It was Nakami. Not the same as I remember her but it was definitely her crazy ass. She was thinner than I had remembered and she'd cut and dyed her hair. I wasn't one hundred percent sure but she looked like she had gotten some plastic surgery done. And although it was weird as fuck seeing the bitch I thought I had killed a year ago, what was even more confusing was the fact that she was clad in expensive lingerie and makeup.

She stood at the stairway with a bright smile on her face like she hadn't called me and confessed that she was going to kill my fiancé. Even though she had lost weight, she was filling out the black, see-through lace one piece that she had on and she had model height due to the Giuseppe Zannoti

Cruel Summer sandals she sported. I started to walk towards her but was stopped by a big bodyguard looking ass nigga that seemed like he had come out of nowhere. He held his hand out to stop me from moving and then looked at Nakami. She nodded her head, and he moved closer to frisk me. I rolled my eyes as he pulled the gun from my waistband and the one from my ankle. I didn't care what that bitch had said; a nigga wasn't coming up in there without a strap.

Nakami frowned as the bodyguard handed her my guns. "Tsk tsk. I just knew that you wouldn't listen."

"Nakami, I ain't got time to fuck with your crazy ass. I got the money now go get Blaze," I said tossing the duffle over towards her feet.

She stepped over the bag without even attempting to open it. Strutting like she thought she was participating in a couture fashion show, she pulled up on me, placing her hands on my chest. I could hear her moan, and she look up at me with her slanted brown eyes.

"Aww, you didn't think it would be that easy, did you?"

Before I could respond, I felt a small prick in my side. Nakami's grin stretched the width of her face as she stepped away from me. My vision immediately started to blur, and my body grew weak. It only took a few more seconds for me to fall unconscious.

Israel
September 2015

"Stay in the car," I whispered to Blu.

"The fuck I look like? If your brother has Kimani in there, I'm going in."

Blu unbuckled her seatbelt and reached for the door. I put my hand on top of hers to stop her. Furious, she turned to me awaiting an answer for my actions.

"He thinks I'm still on his side. If I go in there with you on my fucking arm, he's not going to hesitate to put a bullet in all three of us. You have to trust me. Stay in the car. There's a fully loaded gun under your seat. Once everything is good, I will text you."

Blu's hand still rested rigidly on the door handle.

"Blu, *please*. I know that you probably think that I'm going to double cross you but seriously. You *have* to trust me."

Blu took a deep breath before releasing the grip she had on the door handle. I let out the breath that I didn't realize that I was holding and reached down to recline her seat.

"Don't make any movements. When I let you know everything is all good, then you can come in. Do you know how to use a gun?"

"No," she whispered.

Removing the gun from underneath her seat, I took the safety off so that it would be easier to use.

"Just aim and shoot. You'll probably get some kickback from the force of the gun, especially with this being your first time but if you have to shoot, the main thing is don't hesitate. Ok?"

She nodded her head and another round of tears leaked from her eyes. She had been crying since we left the hotel, no doubt still blaming herself for what my brother had done. I leaned over and kissed her on her forehead and tried to smile.

"Everything is going to be okay. I promise."

I stepped out of the car and walked up to the building that Roman was holding Kimani in. The building was a housing project that had been condemned by the city. They had plans to make the community new again, tearing down the hood and building new condominiums and strip malls. Our father had been one of the investors in the renovation project, and therefore, we were able to get access to the building without much effort. I walked into the far left building, bending down to fit through the wooden boards that had been nailed to the door and walked through the dark and dirty hallway until I came to the apartment that

Roman had mentioned in his text. I knocked three times and waited for him to open up.

My brother greeted me with a grin once he opened the door. "My nigga, my nigga. Come join the fun."

I stepped inside and was not surprised to see Kimani banged up and tied to a chair. His head was down, so I guessed that Roman had slumped him already. The shit fucked with me because I knew things was gone end bad once Grey found out his brother was gone. Blu was going to be fucking devastated. My eyes moved across the room, and that's when I noticed the girl. She was bound and gagged, looking between me and Roman with wide eyes.

"Who the fuck is that?" I asked pointing to the girl. "What you got her here for?"

"You ain't never heard of them one singing bitches? That's Vicious, the lead singer," he said nonchalantly.

"Bro, have you lost your fucking mind?!" I screamed.

Roman turned to look at me with confusion written on his face.

"You got a fucking celebrity tied up in an abandoned apartment building. Grey and Kimani are small time to the public. But her! She's recognized across the world, nigga! Dragging her into this is going to get us killed or locked the fuck up! What were you thinking?"

"I was thinking that I couldn't leave a witness to identify me, bitch! What you getting upset for?"

"Because you not thinking! And that ain't you! I'm the fucking hot head ass nigga that don't use his brain. You're the methodical thinker, and you're fucking up like this? Tell me you understand where I'm coming from bro!"

This shit wasn't making sense to me. Roman was careful and meticulous with his planning. He weighed the risks and the reward and didn't make a decision until he was fully confident that he was going to come out a winner. But behind this Grey shit, he'd lost himself. He was making rookie mistakes; mistakes that even I wouldn't make.

"No, I don't see where you're coming from! The fuck! Why do I have to keep reminding you that our father is dead because of them muthafuckas! That our sister is never going to be able to finish college or a fucking sentence because of them niggas! Our family! They took away our family!" he yelled so hard and fiercely that there were long strands of spit flying from his mouth.

I stepped back and shook my head. I couldn't believe what I was witnessing. This nigga had lost his fucking mind.

I sighed. "We take Grey out, and we lose even more family, man."

That caused Roman to stop and reel back in confusion. His eyebrows knitted and a scowl appeared on his face.

"What?" He stepped closer to me. "What the fuck you just say?"

"They're our brother's man. They're family too."

I had found out right before Blu had dipped on me. Our father's lawyer had reached out to let me know that there was a part of our father's will that hadn't been revealed at the initial reading. He had purposely had his lawyer wait to reveal that we had other siblings until the FEDS had completely finished the case against us. He hadn't known that he was under investigation, but he had planned for it should the day come and he had wanted to make sure that all his children were safe from prosecution before it was known that we were related.

When I found out, I struggled with what to do with the information. I knew that Roman was on the war path, and I wasn't sure that knowing that we were half-brothers would make any difference to him, but it did to me. I pulled out of Roman's plan once I found out and decided that the shit wasn't worth it anymore. I had lost my father and my sister to the bullshit and even though I wasn't a fan of Grey and especially not Kimani, I wasn't trying to fuck with their lives knowing that we were blood.

"Fuck that shit! That makes it even worse! They ratted to the boys knowing that our father was their father? No fucking loyalty! I should shoot this nigga now!"

Before I could stop him, Roman reached for his gun and aimed it at Kimani. Knowing that Kimani wasn't dead yet, caused me to be relieved but only for a second. I'm not sure what the fuck was going through my mind, but my dumb ass hopped right in front of where Kimani sat, Roman's gun now trained on me.

"Roman, bruh. Just..."

"So this is how it's going to be? My own twin going against me? For these muthafuckas you don't even know? You gon' protect them and say fuck your family, nigga? We came out of the same womb, my nigga and you gon say fuck me?" he was screaming so loud that the last of his words came out hoarse.

"I'm protecting you too, man. This is a mistake. There is no way you survive this. You gon go to fucking jail, nigga. Them boys gon come looking for her." I pointed at Vicious, who was now balling her eyes out. "You walk away, and we can forget about this shit. Take the money we have left and rebuild Pop's empire. That's the shit that he would've wanted. Not this."

"Fuck you! You turned against me! Fuck you, man!"

Those were the last words I heard from my brother before bullets erupted and everything went dark.

Grey
September 2015

"Please, no! Please! I'm pregnant."

My eyes fluttered open at the sound of Blaze's distressed voice. They were heavy, my eyelids, but hearing Blaze begging for her life made me determined to open them. Once they were fully open, I saw Blaze on the other side of the room chained to a furnace. She looked surprisingly unharmed, but I could tell that she was scared as fuck. Instantly, my body tried to move so that I could get to her but I quickly realized that I was chained to something too and that made it impossible for me to move.

Suddenly Nakami came into view with a gun pointed at Blaze; hate emanated from her eyes.

"So, everybody can have a baby by you except me, huh Grey?"

"A baby?" I asked, looking a Blaze.

She nodded her head with tears in her eyes.

"I found out a few days before I was shot. In the ambulance, I was slipping in and out of consciousness, but I asked them to keep the pregnancy a part of my sealed medical records. I knew that your instinct would be to protect me and the baby if you had known but I wanted you to find the people that were after you. Your brothers."

"You knew?"

"Yeah, I was coming home to tell you, and that's when I was shot. I'm sorry I didn't tell you about the baby. I just didn't want you to worry."

Emotions engulfed me as I absorbed what Blaze was saying. I was going to be a fucking father. The thought alone caused me to smile, but that was short lived when a bullet pierced the wall right above my head.

"Ain't bout to be no fucking baby shower in this bitch unless it's mine." Nakami seethed.

Keeping the gun trained on me, she shimmied out of her sheer robe, revealing her scantily clad body entirely. I could see the outline of her breasts through the thin material of her bodysuit and her fat pussy lips sat up, and I could see them as clear as day. I turned my head refusing to give her the attention she was looking for.

"Don't act shy. I remember you being very familiar with everything that I have to offer."

"That was before I knew that you were as unbalanced as a homeless bitch's ph levels. Just kill me and get the shit over with, you demented bitch."

I wasn't quite sure what she had planned, but I didn't want no parts of it. I was tired of playing around with her. I would gladly sacrifice my life for Blaze and my unborn child.

"Soon but not yet. First, you're going to give me what I deserve."

"You don't deserve shit but a one-way trip to hell."

Crossing the room, she reached the bed that I was tied to and slapped the shit out of me. I lunged at her but couldn't reach Nakami due to the handcuffs that tied me to the bed. She started to laugh at my efforts to get to her. "You're probably right," she laughed. "But that's not what I was referring to, nigga." She climbed on top of the bed, and I looked at her confused. "You're going to give me a baby."

"Oh hell the fuck nah!" I yelled as I tried to kick that bitch off the bed.

There was no way that I was sticking my dick inside this nutcase. She laughed wildly as I put up a fight and she called for the bodyguard nigga to come into the room. When he appeared, he had foot shackles in his hand, and he walked over to the bed and handed them to Nakami.

"You dizzy bitch! You not getting this D! Fuck that!" I shouted.

"Oh, I'ma get it, and your bitch is going to enjoy the show," she laughed.

I turned my head in the direction of Blaze. I had forgotten that she was in the room that quick. I could see in her face that she was trying to be strong and not let what was happening affect her, but I knew that it was eating her alive. I felt like shit. I should've made sure this bitch was dead a long time ago.

I was yanked out of my thoughts as the bodyguard pulled my legs straight and Nakami shackled them to the bed frame. After they were clamped shut, she waved the bodyguard out of the room and hopped back onto the bed. Running her hands up my legs and onto my thighs, she smiled seductively.

"Finally, we're alone. Well, as close to alone as were going to get. Now, let's get you primed and ready," she smirked.

She grabbed the material by the pockets of my sweats and yanked them down. Her hand flew to my boxers, searching for my package. When she found it, she pulled it out of its hiding place and stroked it. I cringed as I felt myself getting hard from her movements. How could I be turned on by this bitch? She was nuttier than a Planter's factory, and I was still bricking up. I wanted to chalk it up to me being a man and the littlest of shit getting us horny but fuck that. I was sitting here with a hard on behind the chick I despised and in front of my fiancé, no less. I turned to look at Blaze, but she had her eyes closed, tears steadily streaming down her cheeks. I felt fucking helpless.

"Yeah, that's it, daddy. Make that thing jump for me," she commanded before running her long nail along the underside of my dick. Don't you know that muthafucka jumped too? I gritted my teeth.

"You ain't gotta do this. I brought you your money, and you can take that shit and be the fuck up out."

"That money wasn't even for me, baby. That was for Blaze's father/baby daddy. She ran off with a mil of his money years ago, and he came to collect. So please know that money is not the motive. This is about you."

She positioned herself above my lap and slid herself down on my hard dick. I closed my eyes tight because as fucked up as this situation was this crazy chick's pussy was tight and splashy. If felt good as fuck and I hated myself for feeling that way. Nakami let out a moan with my name at the end of it, causing me to immediately turn my head to look at Blaze. She had pulled her knees up to her chest and buried her face there. I was uncomfortable as fuck, and I started moving, trying to shake Nakami off my dick but she rocked with my motions like a trained horse jockey.

"Don't fight me, Grey. Make this easy on yourself. Just relax and give me what I want."

"It don't matter if I nut inside you or not. You gon' be dead tonight and that's a fucking promise."

She leaned forward and pressed her hands against my chest. Shifting all her weight onto me, she bounced her pussy on top of my dick and spoke through her moans.

"I think you're forgetting who has the upper hand here nigga."

She lifted herself up so that her box was hovering over the tip of my dick, and then she let herself fall right on the D, clenching her walls around me as she came down. The fucking stand and slam. I grunted, forcing the moan that was on the tip of my tongue to stay there. I would NOT give this bitch the satisfaction. She smirked at me as she lifted up again and repeated her signature move, causing my face to tighten.

"This pussy feels good don't it?" she whispered.

"Not better than my bitch's," I managed to croak out.

Truth was the shit felt good, damn good. Her pussy was sloppy wet like she was getting increasingly turned on the more we fucked. I wished like hell that my dick would deflate. I thought of any and everything that I could to make it soft, but her shit was trapping a nigga.

"Doubtful. Speaking of that bitch—" She took the gun she had laid on the bed and fired off a shot in Blaze's direction causing her to scream and look up. "Fuck you got your eyes closed for? You round here thinking you bad enough to be stealing men and shit, then you bad enough to watch me fuck yours. Open your eyes!"

Nakami did all that while still riding my dick. She had clenched her muscles around me so tight I could barely move my dick. It wouldn't go soft for shit and that had me frustrated. Now that she was forcing Blaze to watch, the only thing I could do was get this shit over with. So without warning, I thrust myself into Nakami making her eyes shoot open with surprise. Turning away from Blaze, she focused on me, a smile creeping across her face. I wiped that bitch clean off when I hit her with another thrust that I know she felt all in her guts.

"Fuck! Yes, Grey! Give me all of that big dick!"

She closed her eyes tight, and I turned to Blaze. Her tears were drying, and anger was swelling her body. I mouthed, "I'm Sorry" to her and turned back to concentrate on giving Nakami the nut she had been asking for. The sooner I bust, the sooner I could turn the tables and get Blaze and me out of there. So I trained my thoughts on everything that excited me. Blaze marrying a nigga, her having my seed, her pussy…

"Fuccccckkkkkkkk…" I tried to keep my moan to myself, but the nut that I bust was huge.

Nakami hollered out, obviously feeling the effects of her orgasm breaking, but the sound of gunshots drowned her out. Loud commotion was heard outside the room, and I looked around to see what the fuck was going on. Nakami scrambled to hop off the dick and grab her gun, heading in the direction of the noises. A few more gunshots rang out and the familiar sound of a body hitting the ground sounded before a group of people came into view. Even though a nigga's wet dick was out for everyone to see, I had never been more excited to see my people in my life.

Standing in front of me was my squad; Brandin, who was holding a wounded Nakami by her arm, Cope, Mihzani, Jah, Seven, Treach and Keem, guns drawn and mugs on all their faces. I nodded my head towards Blaze, signaling for them to uncuff her first. Mihzani reached into the backpack she'd swung off her back and grabbed out a big ass pair of bolt cutters.

"Damn, how did ya'll niggas get here?" I asked as Keem and Treach came to uncuff me from the bed. I couldn't even call ya'll. Pussy ass nigga had hacked my phone and shit."

"Yeah nigga, we had Dustin hack your shit too. Because you still had it on, we were able to track your location. Figured some shit had gone down when you didn't hit us back, and we couldn't get in touch."

"My niggas."

Once Keem and Treach had unhooked the last metal bracelet, I hopped up from the bed and dapped everybody up. When I reached Nakami, I was about to drop kick her ass, but Blaze tapped me on my shoulder and lightly pushed me out of the way. Before I could stop her, she hauled off and socked the shit out of Nakami, causing her nose to bust wide open.

"I hope your delusional ass rots in hell," she spat.

Nakami smiled like the looney toon that she was before Brandin shook her.

"I saved her for you. You need me to open the warehouse?" he asked me.

"Nah, I got something else in mind. But later for that bitch. Take her to the fly trap and hold her there. I gotta go find my brother and pray that that nigga ain't dead because of me."

Five months later...

Blaze
February 2016

"C'mere, baby," I called out.

Too tired to move too much, I adjusted myself slightly in the bed as I watched her slowly trudge inside my room. Every time I looked at Harmony, I wanted to cry. I didn't know if it was the hormones that were causing me to be emotional; if I was deeply affected by the time we had lost, but every time she was near me I teared up. All the crying that I was doing was probably why she was still scared of me after three months.

After the whole ordeal with Na-koo-koo, Grey had filled me in on my sister bringing Harmony to him at Baron's request, and that he had her in the care of a family friend that he trusted. He grilled me for hours about the shit that Nakami had let slip, and I finally told him everything. I told him about my mother being Baron's bottom bitch and how when I was eleven she ran off with one of her tricks, and he started molesting and beating me. When my body started developing, the beatings slowed but then he started coming into my room at night, forcing himself on me. Eventually, I became his bottom bitch and helped him control his stable of freaks.

The only thing he would allow me to do outside of work for him was attend community college. It was in my second year that I found out that I was pregnant. I was scared and ashamed. I was about to have my father's baby. I was giving birth to my sister. The shit had me so twisted in the head that I remained sick my entire pregnancy. I was on bed rest for eight whole months. The day after I was released from the hospital, I raided his safe and got the fuck out of dodge. I felt bad for leaving Harmony, but I promised myself that I would come back to get her before she became of age and was forced to fulfill Baron's sick fantasies.

Once I filled Grey in, he demanded that we get DNA tests run to ensure that Harmony was my daughter, and Baron was her father. He also said that we should get a DNA test done for me to make sure that I was Baron's daughter. With a mother who turned tricks for a living, I wasn't against it. We ended up having a family outing to the doctor's office because I refused to sleep with Grey again until he got every possible test he could get run after he was forced to have sex with that bitch raw. I didn't think she was dirty, but you couldn't be sure behind a scornful, bitter bitch. His tests came back negative, and I found out that Baron was not my father. He was Harmony's but he wasn't mine, and that was more than a little weight lifted off my shoulders.

"You want to watch K.C. Undercover with me?" I asked Harmony as she hopped into the bed next to me.

"You like that show?" her eyes lit up, and it made me smile.

"I do. I love Zendaya. She's pretty funny, huh?"

Harmony nodded her head, and I turned the remote towards the TV to find the show On Demand.

Grey and I had both gone through some real life scripted TV shit—from the bitch Nakami coming from the dead, and finding out that he had a whole other family, to me finding out that Barron wasn't my father. As much as we loved each other, we mutually decided that it was best to take time to get our emotions together. So, Harmony and I had our own spot, and Grey had his. I wanted nothing more than to be Mrs. Kendrick Summers, but until I was sure that me and my kids' lives wouldn't be affected by that crazy bitch Nakami, I was happy dating him and learning things that I didn't know before about him and his family.

Blu
February 2016

"Okay, now put your hands around your neck, gently. Look at the camera but keep your eyes low. That's it!"

I tried my best to follow the photographer's directions but my body was awkwardly contorted, and it was hard for me to hold my balance. I was only able to hold still for a few frames before I went toppling over. Marquis and Tatum fell out in laughter, and I couldn't help but join in.

"Bitch, you looked like a weeble-wobble. I was wondering how many more instructions you could take before you fell the fuck down!" Marquis howled.

I doubled over in laughter, fresh tears sprouting from my eyes. It felt good to emit tears of happiness for a change. I had cried so much over the past four months that I thought I would be physically sick if I had to shed one more tear.

When we had pulled up to the place where Roman was holding Kimani, in my mind, there was no way that I wasn't going inside that building to get my man. When Israel explained why he needed me to stay behind, it made sense, but I still wasn't having it. As soon as I saw him approach the building, I quietly got out of the car and followed behind him. I heard everything that was said during Israel and

Roman's argument, and when shit got heated, I knew it was
either do or die. I tried to remember how to hold a gun from
when I watched cop shows on TV, but it was way different
when trying to do it yourself. So when I fired my shots, the
kickback caused me to raise my hands higher than where I
was trying to aim, and I shot Israel in the head on accident.
But I didn't stop shooting because I hadn't hit my intended
target. I kept firing. I hit Roman three times in the chest and
Kimani once in the shoulder. Once the smoke and dust
cleared, I checked Kimani to make sure that he was good
and then Israel. Luckily, the bullet only grazed his head, and
he was just a little dazed and confused. I checked Roman's
pulse to make sure that he was dead and then called Grey to
see what the fuck I should do next. I wanted to call the
police, but Kimani urged me to call his brother first before
he passed out from the pain. I couldn't get in touch with
Grey, so I just went through his recent calls, hoping to find
someone that could help us. I lucked up finding Brandin's
number, and he let me know he was with Grey. Once I gave
them the address to where we were, they were on their way.

Grey and his goons rushed over, keeping me on the
phone during the drive to instruct me on how to keep
Kimani awake and alert and how to tend to his wound. Once
they arrived, they gave me the keys to their car and told me

to take Kimani to their private doctor and that they would take care of everything else. I was relieved that Kimani was okay, but after I told him what went down with Israel after he questioned why I had been there in the first place, he told me to get the fuck out.

We hadn't spoken to each other since that day. I called repeatedly. I texted and emailed. I even popped up at his events and his house, but he wasn't fucking with me at all. I couldn't blame him. I had fucked the enemy hours after I had left him while he was sleeping. I had royally fucked up. But after months of pleading, I had finally realized that it was over. Kimani was a thing of the past, and it was my fault.

So I buried myself in work. I had become the face of Marquis' styling company and Tatum's extension line. I had also enrolled in massage therapy school, hoping to open my own day spa one day. I had tried to keep myself hella busy because anytime I wasn't, I thought about Kimani. I missed him immensely, but I knew that it was over, and I had to move on with my life. So that's what I was doing.

Kimani

Life had been crazy since everything had gone down. My career had skyrocketed since Vicious and I's kidnapping story went viral. Grey and I shared full details to our lawyers in hopes that they could keep us out of trouble, and they had done a solid ass job. They worked with my publicist and a few others to spin a story that got Vicious and I a hell of a lot of media attention.

Steph was constantly blowing up my phone about one opportunity or another and Clappers was doing numbers since I had started hosting one night a week. Bitches came out in droves to see the boy in person and the fellas flocked because they knew that the bad ones would be in attendance. The only thing in my life that had been fucked up was Blu.

That girl broke my heart when she told me that had slept with Israel...my own brother, come to find out...after she dipped on a nigga. The fact that she hadn't even wasted time and knew that she was fucking with the enemy had me feeling like the shit she did was unforgivable. But I can't even front. I had been sick without her. All the monetary and superficial success didn't amount to nothing without her and even though she had hurt a brother real bad, I knew that it was partially my fault that she felt the need to do what she did.

I approached the glass door and took a deep breath before I reached for the handle. Nerves were getting the best of me, but I had to man-up and push them aside. I opened the door and walked into the photoshoot. I saw Blu laughing it up with Marquis and Tatum, and the sound of her laughter was like a dope ass 90's R&B song. It was classic, smooth and felt like love. I knew that I was making the right decision. Marquis looked up and in my direction, and I nodded. He smiled wide before breaking eye contact and taking Blu over to the computer where the images from the shoot were being displayed.

Marquis positioned her behind the computer screen. "Come here, goofy girl and help me pick out the best ones."

I watched as they ooh'd and aah'd over the photos she'd taken until a confused expression crossed Blu's face. She hit the keyboard trying to get to the next picture, but I knew that the screen had frozen.

"What happened, Quis?" she asked.

"Girl, you done broke the photographer's shit. Can't take black people nowhere. Move, child." He pushed her out of the way and pressed a button on the computer making the screen go black. Usher's "There Goes My Baby" eased out of the speakers connected to the laptop. Blu looked up in confusion. I made sure to hide in the background so that she couldn't see me.

My pre-recorded voice came flowing out of the Beat's Pill that Tatum was now holding. "I never thought that I could love again...'til I met Blu. I met her at the grand opening of my brother's club, and when I laid eyes on her, I thought that she was the most beautiful thing to ever grace the earth. She knocked me off my feet."

Blu looked in the direction of the recording, and when they landed on Tatum, her facial expression looked like a big question mark.

"I pursued her, but I could tell that she was hesitant to open up. To let me in. Slowly but surely, I knocked down those walls. Blu was tough to crack. She refused to give herself enough credit. She refused to believe that she was worthy of love, and I was determined to prove her wrong."

On cue, a swarm of people entered the room carrying large bouquets of flowers. There was every single type of flower you could imagine: Tulips, roses, daisies, lilies, poppies, hyacinths, calla lilies, peonies, hydrangeas, and orchids; all in different shades of blue. I watched as tears welled up in Blu's eyes and her hands flew to her mouth. She searched the room for me, but I wasn't ready yet.

"At one point, I thought that I lost her. And then again, I thought that I pushed her away. And although both times were because of different things, the result was the same. I was sick without her. A nigga couldn't eat or sleep the same. Hell, it was hard for me to breathe the same without her presence. We've been through some shit, but my love for her overrules any situation we could every encounter. Good, bad or ugly, I just want my Blu back."

Finally, I came out of my hiding spot and came into view. The butterflies that danced in my stomach increased with each step I took towards Blu. I was clean as fuck thanks to Marquis hooking me up with the Armani Collezioni tuxedo and black bowtie. On my feet was a pair of sick ass Corthay red and black patent leather dress shoes. Blu matched my fly in her deep red, strapless Monique Lhulilier gown that I had picked out. I had never seen her this dressed up, but she was beyond gorgeous. She had gotten all dolled up at my expense, but she'd thought that she was doing a shoot for Tatums's hair collection. Her friends had really come through for a nigga, helping me set up the fake shoot, the recording, and the flowers. We had been working on this shit for damn near two weeks. Tatum had her hair flowing down her back, and her make-up was on point. She looked beautiful.

I approached Blu, who was still crying her eyes out. Both Tatum and Marquis had tears in their eyes too. I chuckled nervously before I dropped down to one knee. I grabbed a hyperventilating Blu's hand.

"Fuck everything in the past, baby. I'm over that shit. I can't go another day without you by my side. You're my rib. The other piece of me and I can't live the rest of my life unless I know that I'll be living it with you."

I reached down into my pocket and pulled out the ring box. Licking my lips…a nervous habit…I popped the box open to reveal the 8 karat, light pink, diamond ring in the rose gold diamond halo setting. Gasps were heard around the room once the ring was revealed. I was glad because I had worked on this ring for about a month with a jeweler from Italy to make it unique.

"I'm asking you in the humblest way possible to spend a couple of forever's with a nigga. Blu Buckley, will you marry me?"

"Yes," she whispered.

My heart swelled as I slipped the ring on her finger. "What? I can't hear you?"

"Yes!" she said louder.

I stood to my feet. "Well scream that shit then, Blu baby," I grinned.

"Yes, Kimani Summers, I'll marry you!" she screamed at the top of her lungs.

A round of applause sounded off as well as camera flashes. I pulled my fiancé by her waist and brought her to my body. I kissed her like I was trying to make amends for every mistake any man had ever made against her. I pulled back from the kiss eventually. Blu's eyes remained closed, still in a daze. I kissed both of her eyelids and then whispered in her ear.

"I love you, Blu."

"I love you too, baby."

My life was finally complete.

Grey
February 2016

"We good to come through?" I asked into the phone.

I got the affirmative from the person on the other end of the phone and ended the call. I looked over at Blaze as I placed my hand on her thigh.

"You sure you want to do this?" I asked her.

She nodded her head without hesitation. "I need to be sure."

I nodded and placed the car in drive, pulling out of the airport parking lot. We had just landed in Detroit, and I was glad to be able to put everything behind me and move on. Blaze and I's relationship had been slowed to a snail's pace because of the shit that went down with Nakami, and I was ready to make my family official. I needed her to see that I was serious when I said that situation was handled. I had enjoyed getting to know Blaze all over again, but I was ready to marry my baby.

Things in my life had changed, and they had stayed the same. My businesses were booming like they had been before. After Midnight had taken flight without effort and I was thinking about opening another location in Detroit and Atlanta. South Beach was popping as usual, and I was booking events left and right. My illegal shit was still tight, and I was moving weight faster than Hero ever did. And Blaze didn't know it, but I was in the process of getting her a building in Beverly Hills to open her second location.

Roman's death was inevitable, but it was still crazy. He'd really gone off the deep end, and it was unfortunate that his brother couldn't talk him off the ledge. Israel was fucked up about it but in the process of losing one brother, he had gained two more. We weren't tight, but we were getting there. It was hard to bond with all the shit from the past was still pretty fresh. We tried to meet regularly but life sometimes got in the way, and it was still painful for Israel sometimes so we let that nigga rock. I low-key thought that he still felt some type of way about Blu choosing Kimani over him, but whatever. He was trying to get over it.

Thirty minutes later, we pulled up to a nice looking apartment complex in Canton. I pulled up in the assigned parking space and parked the car. unlocking the doors. Blaze and I hopped out of the car. I walked on the other side and grabbed her hand, kissing it and then intertwining my fingers through hers. We walked up the stairs to apartment number 135, and I used my key to unlock the door.

"Butter? You in here?!" I shouted.

Butter came bouncing out of the back room dressed in a form fitting dress and a lab coat, glasses resting on her nose. She smiled when she saw Blaze and I, then came forward to give us each a hug.

She walked towards the room that she had originally come from. "In here."

We followed behind her and entered the room. Blaze immediately gasped, and I shook my head. Instead of killing her like I was tempted to that night, I had handed Nakami off to Butter and let her use her to test the new drug she was using. And seeing her right now, confirmed that I had made the correct decision.

Nakami was a shell of her former self. The drugs had taken everything from her. Her beauty, her body and what was left of her mind. She lay in the bed in a daze, staring off into space with a blank look in her eyes. Her eyes were sunken in, and she had lost a ton of weight. Her lips were dry, and she kept nodding her head like she was hearing music, but the room was silent. She had been under Butter's care for the entire three months getting hooked on whatever it was that Butter was cooking up, and it looked like it was lethal because Nakami was gone. She didn't even bother acknowledging us when we came into the room.

"The whole apartment building is soundproof. Do what you gotta do. Good seeing you both." Butter smiled brightly and placed a .45 on the dresser near the door before she walked out.

"What did you do to her?" Blaze whispered. I could see tears forming in her eyes.

"Butter is making a new drug. She needed someone to test it on to see the side effects. I thought she would be perfect," I smirked.

Silence fell between us as Blaze watched Nakami. Her tears now made their way down her face.

"Is she done? With the drug?" she asked hesitantly.

I stared at Nakami, studying her. She looked bad, worse than a crackhead or a meth head. Whatever Butter was whipping up was crazy.

"Yeah I believe so. She—"

My sentence was cut off by the sound of the gun going off. The bullet shot straight through Nakami's head, causing her head to snap back against the wall. Blood and brain matter splattered all across the stark white room. I turned to face Blaze, who held the .45 in her hands. I hadn't even seen her pick it up. She was still staring at Nakami; her eyes now void of the tears that had just been there.

"I had to be sure." She whispered.

I took the gun from her trembling hands and put it down on the dresser, then grabbed her in a bear hug. That chapter was finally closed. It was going to take some time to get Blaze past what happened, but she could rest easy now. All my demons were gone, and she now knew without a shadow of a doubt, she was the only one I would ever belong to.

THE END!

Made in the USA
Charleston, SC
10 December 2016